3060

MW01109481

THE
GUNFIGHTER'S
APPRENTICE

THE GUNFIGHTER'S APPRENTICE

•

Jerry S. Drake

AVALON BOOKS
NEW YORK

Published by Thomas Bouregy & Co., Inc.
160 Madison Avenue, New York, NY 10016

Library of Congress Cataloging-in-Publication Data

Drake, Jerry S.
The gunfighter's apprentice / Jerry S. Drake.
p.   cm.
ISBN 0-8034-9790-3 (acid-free paper)
I. Title.

PS3604.R35G86   2006
813'.6—dc22
2005034634

PRINTED IN THE UNITED STATES OF AMERICA
ON ACID-FREE PAPER
BY HADDON CRAFTSMEN, BLOOMSBURG, PENNSYLVANIA

For Virginia and three special daughters,
Peggy, Susan and Nancy.

Prologue

The young clerk stopped sweeping the floor in the corner and turned at the sound of the bell over the door. Three unkempt young men sauntered into the store, scuffing their boots as they walked and making deliberate, intrusive sounds. He'd seen the trio earlier in the day through the window of the store; loud-mouthed ruffians, swearing and being obnoxious, brushing men and women from the sidewalks as they passed. They'd been roaming the streets of the frontier community and making nuisances of themselves. He wondered why they hadn't been arrested or, at least, run out of town.

Troublemakers.

Now, they shuffled through the aisles, pushing at the displays of leather goods at the front of the store, upsetting stacks of woolens and cotton garments either through drunken carelessness or deliberation. For a few moments, they'd amused themselves by trying on

1

women's hats, then tossing them to the floor as they wandered toward the hardware section.

"Anybody here?" called the one at the head of the pack, his voice loud and demanding, his words slightly slurred. He was a slim, dark-clad youngster with an arrogant manner. "Where the hell is the damned storekeep?"

"Ain't nobody here, Jared," said another of the trio. "Let's go back over to the bar."

The clerk laid the broom aside and moved out of the shadows to stand behind the back counter, his right hand at his side just above the loaded shotgun that was propped below the counter, barrel pointed down. "Something I can do for you?"

The three young men turned and ambled toward him. "Where the hell have you been hiding?" the young leader, Jared, asked. "We come in here, maybe we're going to buy out the store and you laying back there taking a nap, I reckon." He looked back at his two companions, seeking their approval of his insolence.

"I think you gentlemen should come back at another time," the clerk said, his hand grasping the shotgun, his finger hovering just above the trigger guard. "We're getting ready to close."

"We?" the arrogant young man swept his eyes around the store. "I don't see any 'we.' All I see is you."

"Make it another day."

"Do good business today, storekeep?"

The clerk remained silent.

"Maybe you'd better show us all your money, storekeep," Jared said, his hand dropping to the holstered gun on his hip. "Bet it's a bundle."

The clerk brought the shotgun up into view, aiming

it at the hooligan's chest. Behind him, the other two stepped backward, looking to run. The young man's eyes opened in surprise. He regarded the barrel of the shotgun, then looked up, a smile of scorn spreading on his lips. "I don't think so, storekeep." His hand swept his handgun out and up to trigger a shot directly at the clerk's head.

Chapter One

"Two men coming!"

The young woman at the bedroom door, still in her nightgown, had been up for a couple of hours, restless. She'd been cleaning the ranch house as best she could, picking up and straightening things, moving softly so as not to wake her companion. He'd been aware of her even as he'd dozed, unable to decide whether to curl deeper into sleep to relieve the piercing hangover or to pull her down to him the next time she crept into the small bedroom.

"Not far away," she called again, urgently. "Coming up from Gold Stream."

Tom Patterson threw the coverlet aside, swung out of bed and reached for the Winchester in the nearby corner. The tall, muscular man strode barefoot and bare-assed through the door into the living room, not at all concerned about his nakedness.

4

"My God, Tom!" the woman said in dismay. "Put your pants on!"

Ignoring her, he stepped through the side door and crouched low behind the weathered and broken split rails that had, for a long ago tenant, protected a small garden. He moved to one of the posts and laid the rifle barrel at the joint of the cross rail, taking casual aim at the two figures approaching on horseback.

From the distance of a quarter mile down the pass, he could see the riders coming up the aspen-lined mountain trail, one on an iron-gray horse and the other on a roan. Both men were dressed in somber suits and wearing bowler hats. As they came onto the mountain meadow, he could see that one was large, portly and middle-aged, bouncing against the rhythmic gait of his dusky mount. The younger man was too similarly dressed not to be, in some way, related.

No one Tom recognized. *Not likely to be a threat. Still. . . .*

"I'll take them pants now, Betty," he called.

The woman took a tentative step out of the door, self-consciously tying a wrapper around her, carrying Tom's pants over her arm. "Here!" she said as she thrust them at him. "It wasn't decent, you coming out without a stitch."

" 'Drather be caught with my britches clean off than half-down," he said with wry humor. Without taking his eyes from the oncoming riders, Tom leaned the rifle against the rail and stepped one leg, then the other, into his trousers. He fastened the buttons up to the waist, sucking in his stomach, straining at the pooch below his belly button that made fastening a task. He retrieved the rifle and held it at the ready across his chest, high enough that the riders would see it.

"Mr. Patterson?" came a distant hail from the older man. "With your permission, we'd like to come in!"

"Whaddya want here?" Tom called back.

The two men reined up and leaned together to confer. Then, the older man turned again to face the house. "We're here to talk business! You *are* Tom Patterson, are you not?"

"What kind of business?" Tom shouted back.

"To your benefit, Mr. Patterson!" came the shouted reply. "It will bring you a good sum of money!"

"What kind of business?" Tom bellowed again.

For a moment, there was silence.

"Do we have to shout about it?" came the irritated cry, the older man's temper showing as he wheeled his gray horse and moved toward the house, reining up again after a few steps. "My name is Ezra McKay!" he exclaimed loudly, then gestured to the younger man. "This is my son, Matthew!" He paused again. "We're not up to any mischief, Mr. Patterson! We're business people from Nebraska City! People can vouch for us!"

"I don't want to buy anything!" Tom shouted. "I ain't got a goddamned dime to my name, so if that's your business, jes' keep on riding!"

"You don't understand, Mr. Patterson!" the elder McKay replied. "I've come with a proposition to your benefit!"

Tom turned to the young woman, a lopsided grin on his unshaved face. "A proposition?" he said, cocking his head in puzzlement. "What the hell does he mean by that?"

"We ain't going to find out here yelling across all creation," she said. "Why don'cha let 'em come on in, Tom? Damned if I wouldn't blame 'em if they'd jes' ride back where they came from."

"Let 'em," Tom said, nodding. He raised the rifle to his shoulder, training the sights on the oldest man. "I'd take your boy and ride on, Mr. McKay!" he shouted. "Don't mean to be hard about it, but I don't like strangers even if they're wearing suits and carrying their bona fides!"

"Tom, for God's sake!" Betty fussed behind him. "You could try to be polite." She stared at the men. "They look all right to me."

"Rode with a fella named Arlo Fairchild," Tom said, as much to himself as to her. "Preacher in a buggy came to his house one day, carrying a Bible. Wanted Fairchild to kneel with him and pray. Arlo bowed his head and the preacher shot him in the chin before they got to 'Amen.'" He looked to the woman, then shrugged. "I'll let 'em come into the yard, but you git into the house. There's an old Henry rifle in there, already loaded. If shooting starts, you just start banging away at 'em."

"Lordy, Tom," she protested. "There ain't going to be any trouble. You can just tell that by looking at 'em." Then she gave a short laugh. "'Sides, I don't know much about shooting any rifle."

"If they've come to shoot me, they ain't likely to let you walk away and talk about it," he warned.

Then, with another shrug, he waved the rifle to beckon them in. "Well, come on in, Mr. McKay! Come slow and hold your reins up high where I can see your hands!"

Again, the two men leaned together to talk, the younger man appearing to resist, their distant pantomime revealing a demanding father and a reluctant yet compliant son.

"We're not carrying weapons, Mr. Patterson!" Ezra McKay called out. "Not on our persons, in our saddlebags."

"They'd be damned handy if you needed 'em," Tom muttered in contempt, loud enough for Betty to hear as she started for the house. "Come on in! We'll talk right here over the fence!"

Tom watched the McKays carefully as they spurred their horses into a walk toward the house. As they came nearer, he saw that Ezra McKay was a big, rotund man, somewhere between fifty and sixty, his girth making his age anyone's guess. He didn't look comfortable on his horse; a buggy would've suited him better. The young McKay, riding stiffly, was about twenty, Tom thought. He appeared a trim and sturdy youngster with a nearly handsome face, probably the spitting image of his father at an earlier age. They were town people, too proper to shed their suit coats even though the Colorado sun was high in the sky now, driving the mountain cool back to the shadows.

They looked harmless enough, but Tom kept a fence post between them and him. He glanced back at the house and nodded in approval as he saw Betty holding the Henry just inside the door.

"You don't need to git down," Tom told them as they

reined up at the fence. "Spread them coats open, if you please."

Obediently, both men laid their reins on their saddle horns and opened their coats. "You're a suspicious man, Mr. Patterson," McKay said.

"You're right about that," Tom agreed gruffly. "What do you fellas want?"

A man accustomed to taking charge, McKay leaned forward to speak: "We run a general store over in Nebraska City, never had a bit of trouble in nearly ten years starting back in '64. We run an honest business and we've done pretty well. Matt, here, worked at the store as a boy and, now, as a young man. He'll likely continue in my place when my time comes."

Tom coughed to signal his impatience.

"I see you want to get right to the matter, Mr. Patterson," McKay said. "Very well." He gave a nod to his son. "A few weeks ago, three young rowdies decided to rob the store late on a Saturday afternoon. I wasn't there, but Matt was." He paused for a moment and nodded to his son once again. "Matt guessed what they were up to and got a shotgun on them. One of them pulled a gun and shot at him and Matt shot back." He stopped and shrugged. "Unfortunately for Matt, the man died."

Tom considered this. "Seems to me like it was more unfortunate for the other fella."

"The name Moss mean anything to you?" McKay asked.

Tom shrugged.

"Jack Moss?"

Tom looked at the two of them with skepticism. "Are

you saying," he gestured with his rifle to Matt McKay, "that he shot Jack Moss?"

"Jared Moss," the elder McKay explained, "his younger brother."

Tom gave a wry smile. "Jack probably won't like that."

The father nodded. "From what I've been told, he's a vicious killer. If and when he finds out about his brother, I'm of the opinion that he will try to get even."

Tom gave the statement some thought, then nodded in agreement. "I'd say that's probably jes' what he'll do."

Behind him, Tom heard Betty come out through the side door. He glanced back at her and saw that she carried the Henry carelessly by her side, her curiosity walking her forward.

The elder McKay, then the younger, tipped their hats to her. "Good morning, Mrs. Patterson," McKay said politely. "Sorry to disturb your morning."

Betty glanced at Tom with a nervous, guilty smile.

"What's all this got to do with me?" Tom asked.

McKay drew a deep breath, as though to say something he'd been practicing: "Well, we've been to the law and they tell us that they'll try to keep their eyes open in case Jack Moss shows up, but that's hardly any comfort. Someday, someplace, Moss will surely catch up with Matt . . . and the boy would be no match for him." He waited to see if Tom understood, then made it clear in case he didn't. "People tell me that you're better than average with a gun."

Tom made no response.

"I'd like to hire you to teach the boy to protect himself."

Tom turned his attention to Matthew McKay, appraising him. "You always let your pa do all the talking?"

The young man's head turned sharply and, for an instant, resentment flared in his eyes. "Most of the time, he does," he responded with some bitterness. "Whether I like it or not."

McKay gave his son an annoyed glance, then took over the discussion once again. "I'd like to make you a business proposition, Mr. Patterson. Pay you to teach Matt how to handle a gun, maybe some of the tricks he'd need to have a chance against—"

"Ain't likely to work," Tom interrupted with an impatient shake of his head. " 'Sides, I'm outta that sort of thing now. Folks have a way of embroidering the truth, making out that I'm some sort of a gunfighter."

"You've had a reputation as a lawman as I recall," McKay began. "I thought—"

"Jes' fer the record, I've worked both sides of the law," Tom cut in again. "You ought to know that. I ain't no do-gooder so don't you go making me out as such."

McKay considered, and then acknowledged the statement with a slow nod.

"And I don't know that what worked for me would ever work for your boy," Tom continued. He looked at Matt with a steady and almost insulting stare. "You had a shotgun on the man and he drew on you before you got off a shot?"

"If you want the straight of it, he fired twice," Matt

replied in an measured, detached manner, taking off his bowler hat to touch his temple. At the edge of his blond hairline, a faint red mark was still visible. "Second one grazed me. That's when I fired." Without further comment, he replaced the hat and returned Tom's steady gaze with something that resembled defiance.

Tom turned away to face the father.

"It's worth two hundred and fifty dollars to me, Mr. Patterson," McKay said with some pomposity. He glanced around the rundown ranch, examining the log house with the forlorn front porch, the ramshackle outbuildings, dilapidated barn and tumbledown horse corral. "You own this place, Mr. Patterson?"

"Don't know that that's any of your business," Tom responded.

"Two hundred and fifty dollars would go a long way to fixing it up," McKay continued. "It'd be a really pretty place if you had the wherewithal to do something with it."

"You don't understand, Mr. McKay," Tom said. "It ain't the money." He nodded toward Matt. "He don't look like he's got the heart for it." He paused for a few moments. "You'd be better off using that money to hire someone to take care of Jack Moss."

The elder McKay didn't understand immediately and, when he did, conflicting emotions played across his face; a twitch of temptation instantly replaced by a frown of distaste. "I wouldn't hire murder, Mr. Patterson," he said with low intensity.

"Well, suit yourself," Tom said. "You may think different when it's over and done." With a gesture of dismissal, he half-turned toward the ranch house, motioning Betty ahead of him.

"Five hundred!"

Tom turned back with a sigh. "You're making it mighty hard to say no, Mr. McKay."

"It's either you or somebody else," McKay told him. "You got the edge right now because we don't have a lot of time and I don't know where else to go, but I will find someone who'll help him." He waited for Tom's reaction. "Seven-fifty."

Tom glanced from the older man to the son, sizing him up once again, unable to come to a conclusion. "What do you say?" he asked young McKay.

Matt returned the stare. "I didn't know that I was to have any part in the conversation." Then, he looked away to his father. "Wouldn't it be better for all concerned if I just left this part of the country?"

Tom smiled and nodded his approval. "Now, that makes a whole lot of sense." He looked at the older man. "He's right. Use your money to send your boy back East till this thing blows over."

"And when would that be?" McKay questioned. "Two years? Five? Ten?"

"Hell," Tom swore in vexation, "he wouldn't ever have to come back, would he? He could make a living—"

"And what would happen to our store and our lives?" McKay interrupted with some derision. "What would happen to all the years that I've spent building it up for him?"

"Hell, I thought you was worried about your boy, not your goddamned store," Tom said.

"One thousand dollars, Mr. Patterson," McKay said bluntly. "My absolute last offer. That's as high as I can possibly go. You can take it or leave it."

Tom frowned and pursed his lips and cast another appraising glance at Matt, then looked to his father. "Cash in advance?" he asked.

"Half now, the other half when the job's done to our satisfaction," McKay countered.

"I hope that don't mean after a showdown with Jack Moss," Tom said, not really in jest. "All right, I'll expect the rest when I bring him back and I say he's ready as he's ever gonna be."

"Bring him back?" McKay questioned in surprise. "I thought you'd be coming back with us."

Tom shook his head. "'Drather it'd be here. We go to Nebraska City and we'd be looking over our shoulders for Jack Moss to come in." He gestured to the dilapidated ranch house. "We got a spare room for him here and it'd take some time for Moss to find him. If I'm gonna do him any good, I'd jes' as soon be working in my own place and using whatever I got that might be of some help." He looked at Matt McKay. "That all right with you?"

The young man shrugged. "I suppose so," he replied, his answer almost beneath hearing. "Whatever the two of you say."

"You got extra clothes?" Tom asked, a deprecating gesture at the young man's dark suit. "Something ordinary?"

Matt bobbed his head at the saddle pack behind him. "I got a couple of changes in there. I suppose they'll do till I get into Gold Stream."

Tom stood expressionless for a while, then nodded and motioned him toward the barn. "You can put your horse and tack in the barn while your pa and I do a little business."

The young man shot an oblique look at his father and, at the older man's slight nod, gave a gesture of tired compliance and spurred the roan toward the barn.

As soon as he was out of earshot, Tom voiced his doubt again. "I really don't know, Mr. McKay." He looked at Matt as the young man dismounted and led his horse into the open door of the barn, giving the animal a soothing caress as he did. "Ain't nothing to be ashamed of, but he strikes me as more of a gentle boy and there's not a lot to be done about that." He clucked and shook his head. "He's gotta have some mean in him to do what you aim for him to do."

"It won't do any harm to drill that into him, Mr. Patterson," the father said. "The Lord knows I've really tried." Then, with a grimace at his own words, he softened his manner, looking in Matt's direction, a slight affection showing in spite of stern intent. "He does take more after his mother's temperament than mine," he explained. "He just needs to be a little stronger, a little tougher."

"I can't guarantee nothing," Tom protested.

"Then you've got five hundred dollars for your trouble," McKay said with finality. "Your decision, sir?"

Tom looked toward the barn. "Already made that,

Mr. McKay," he sighed. "We'll see what we can do."
He looked up at the man. "Now . . . about that down
payment."

In answer, McKay reached inside his coat pocket and
pulled out a large wallet, opened it and counted out bills.

"God Almighty!" Tom exclaimed. "You carrying that
much cash on you?"

McKay nodded, closed the wallet and replaced it in
his coat. "I didn't figure a man like you would take anything less than cash," he said matter-of-factly. He
leaned forward to hand the money to Tom.

"If you're carrying any more," Tom advised him,
"I'd dig them weapons out where I could get to 'em in
a hurry."

"There's not that much left, Mr. Patterson," McKay
told him with a wry smile. "It's just about all the ready
cash I could raise in a short time."

Tom fanned the bills to be reassured of the amount,
then placed them into his pants pocket. He nodded
toward the house. "You want to stay to eat before you
head back? To say good-bye to your boy?"

McKay shook his head and then laid his rein hand
out to turn the horse to the side. "Saying good-bye
wouldn't be comfortable for Matt or me," he said. He
cocked his head in a gesture of weary discouragement.
"We don't get along too well," he explained. "He
doesn't like this idea any more than he likes most any
other of mine." He paused. "I love the boy, Mr.
Patterson, but I have a hard time showing it and it'll
take time for him to understand that." He paused again.
"I'm counting on you to give us that time, Mr.
Patterson."

The elder McKay touched the brim of his bowler in a farewell salute, then turned his horse and rode away. As he headed across the meadow, he appeared a nearly comic fat man spurring his animal into a canter, bouncing his way back toward the mountain pass.

Betty came up beside him, watching McKay's departure. "If that don't beat all. Did he really give you all that money?"

In answer, Tom took the bills from his pocket, showed them to her, then stuffed them inside again. "Tell nobody in town, you hear?"

"You think anybody in town would try to come get it?" she teased.

"And don't you go telling anybody why the boy's here either," he commanded. "Can I count on you, Betty?"

"How you gonna explain him, Tom? And the money?" she asked, nodding in hesitant agreement to his question. "People are gonna want to know."

"Don't need to tell 'em a damned thing," Tom said. "Let 'em guess if they've got a mind to."

Young McKay came out of the barn into the sunlight, carrying his saddle pack, his gaze fixed on his now-distant father who was bouncing down the rough trail. He watched for several moments, then turned and started toward the house. As he approached them, he gave a courteous nod to Betty, then directed a question to Tom. "Where do you want me to put my things?"

"There's a spare bedroom," Tom directed with a nod to the ranch house. "Mattress might be kinda dusty, but she'll sleep okay. Jes' make yourself comfortable."

With a gesture of appreciation, Matt moved past

them and stepped onto the porch at the main entrance to the house.

"Seems like a nice boy," Betty said, looking after him.

"That's so," Tom replied. "I'm feared that's gonna be his problem."

Chapter Two

Matt paused a few steps inside the front door of the ranch house to let his eyes adjust from the bright sunlight to the comparative gloom of the interior. It was spacious for a log structure, a large rectangular main room with windows on either side of the door he'd entered. It was a sturdy building, the spruce logs neatly fit together in the inverted saddle method and with a flagstone floor throughout. There was a stone fireplace in the center of a long sidewall with a door and a window just beyond. On the other side of the main room, an L-shaped partition enclosed two small bedrooms. Between the end of the partition and the far wall, there was an open space for eating that contained a slab table and four ladder-back chairs.

Even as large and spacious as the building's interior appeared, without curtains at the windows, cluttered and sparsely furnished with tattered upholstered chairs and rough-hewed tables, it seemed more a shelter than a home.

The far end of the building housed an open kitchen with an iron cookstove and cooking utensils hanging from pegs on the wall nearby. A short log partition jutted out from the wall to enclose a pantry with shelves of canned goods and supplies visible through the open door.

In the main room partition, a door ajar revealed a bedroom, the bed rumpled and covers tossed. A second, closed door indicated an adjacent bedroom at the front of the house. Matt walked to it and pushed it open. As he stepped inside, the smell of stale air wrinkled his nose. He stood for several seconds, then raised a billow of dust by plopping his saddle pack on the narrow bed. He moved to the single small window, battled to open it, and was rewarded by a faint breeze, which barely stirred the musty air of the tiny bedroom. He glanced at the door and decided that occupancy might just be endurable if the door was left open to circulate that small current through the room.

He stepped back to his saddle pack, unfastened it and started placing his few garments on pegs in the wall, his shaving mug, brush, toothbrush, and smaller belongings on a single wall shelf. Stashing his saddle pack in the corner of the room, he turned to the bed and pulled back the dusty coverlet to inspect the mattress. From the misshaped look of it, sleep wouldn't come easy for the duration of his stay.

"Let me find you a better blanket," came the woman's voice from behind him.

Matt turned as Betty entered the room.

"Sorry, there ain't no sheets," she apologized. She

took the coverlet from him and wadded it up as though to remove it quickly from his sight. "I'll get you a pillow if I can find one." She nodded her head at the bed. "I don't 'spect it'll be too comfortable, but it ought to be clean, ain't got no bugs in it or anything. Ain't nobody slept there for a long time." She turned to him with a bright smile. "Let me air it out awhile."

"I'm sure it'll be fine, ma'am," Matt said hurriedly. "No need to bother."

"No bother at all," she responded. "We'll put it out on the front porch where the sun is."

Matt moved quickly to grasp the mattress in the middle and took it on his shoulders. "Show me the way."

She smiled at him and walked ahead through the main room and opened the front door to lead him out. On the porch, she gestured to a still-standing section of the railing. "Right on that there rail or what's left of it."

Matt placed the mattress on the rail and positioned it so the sun would fully shine upon it.

"Might come out in a couple of hours and do the other side," the woman counseled. "Ought to take any damp out." She turned to go back inside. "We ain't had our breakfast yet," she said apologetically. "I 'spect it'd be more your noonday meal, wouldn't it?"

"Don't go to any trouble—"

"No trouble at all," she broke in. "Lordy, boy, fixing for you ain't no more than doing the same for Tom."

"That would be very nice of you," he said. "Thank you, ma'am."

They walked inside and Betty moved directly to the kitchen where she busied herself lighting a fire in the black iron cookstove. Matt, ill at ease, pondered whether to stay inside and talk to the woman or to seek out Patterson.

Patterson came inside, walked to the table and sat down on one of the chairs.

Matt overcame his hesitancy and walked over to join him. "Any idea of how long I'm going to be here, Mr. Patterson?"

Tom gave him an indifferent glance. "None at all," he answered gruffly.

"A few days? A couple of weeks?" Matt persisted.

Patterson showed his annoyance with a petulant scowl. "I just told you I don't have no idea. It ain't the sort of thing I've ever done. I gotta do some thinking on how to go about it."

"Don't let last night's booze make you nasty, Tom," Betty scolded, then addressed Matt. "He'll be a sight better later on in the day when he ain't hungover."

"We won't get started on it today if that's what you got in mind," Patterson said to him. "I got to do some figgering."

"Whatever you say," Matt responded.

They ate their breakfast in relative silence, only Betty making an occasional comment, her subdued manner matching Matt's in the company of their grumpy companion. For his part, Patterson seemed to be nearly unaware of them, his head down as he concentrated on the food on his plate. He forked down fried potatoes, bacon, biscuits and honey, making no eye contact with either the woman or his new houseguest.

After the meal, without a word, he disappeared into the bedroom and closed the door.

Betty rose and cleared the table, then began to wash dishes.

"Anything I can do?" Matt asked.

"Not a thing," she responded. "You might bring in that mattress. It ought to be sun-dried by now. Or you can just take it easy. I 'spect Tom will be taking a nap for a while."

Matt glanced at the closed door. "I thought I might be able to help Mr. Patterson with some of his chores."

She smiled at the notion. "Tom ain't big for doing much around the place." She glanced around the cabin. "Lord knows something's got to fall down on top of him before he gets around to doing any chores."

"What's he do during the day?"

"Just about what has to be done and nothing more," she replied with a faint smile. "You could call him lazy."

"I think I could," Matt said in amused agreement.

"I don't think I would to his face," Betty cautioned, still in good humor. "Especially not today, way he's feeling."

"Well, I got to do something," Matt complained. "Suppose he'd mind if I did some work around the place?"

"No, I don't suppose so," she responded. "Just don't be too noisy about it." She frowned in thought. "I 'spect he wouldn't mind if you'd cut some firewood for the cookstove and brought it in." She gestured to the barn. "You'll find an ax out there." She pointed in a different direction. "There's a stand of birch out there where he sometimes does some cutting. He'd probably appreciate you doing that for him."

Matt nodded and walked out the front door, retrieved the mattress, and returned it to his bedroom. He moved outside again and headed toward the barn. Inside, he looked around in the shadows and found a number of tools stacked carelessly in one corner. Most were in sorry condition; spades, axes, and shovels with rusted metal and splintery wood shafts. He selected the better of two axes, tested the blade with his thumb and grunted a grudging satisfaction. Nonetheless, he continued to search the cobwebbed recesses until he found a whetstone.

With the ax and whetstone, he walked out of the barn and headed for the distant grove of trees, seeing that three had been felled. He began to apply the whetstone to the edge of the ax, stroking it smoothly, rhythmically, casting an occasional glance at the distant ranch house.

What have I got myself into?

Chapter Three

The next morning, Betty fixed breakfast for the two men, washed the dishes, then disappeared into the bedroom she'd shared with Tom, leaving them in the awkward silence that had prevailed since young McKay's arrival.

The evening before had been strained. Uncomfortable in strange quarters, Matt had been troubled by all the drinking and the surprisingly ribald relationship between the couple. After the evening meal, as if he wasn't there, they'd carried on, working their way through the better part of a bottle of bourbon. Tom had been caressing her and running his hand up her dress while she, giggling, encouraged it. Early on, embarrassed, he'd excused himself, walking through the living room to his cramped, stifling bedroom. With nothing to do, he'd spent a couple of lonely hours before sleeping, hearing drunken laughter and clear sounds of carnal scramblings in the adjacent bedroom.

It had been a long night.

"Ever do any shooting?" Tom growled across the kitchen table, his words slurred from the whiskey of the night before, almost unintelligible through his mouthful of hoecake. "Other than shotgunning Jared Moss?"

The young man ignored the insolent remark. "Not much," he replied. "We do stock shotguns, rifles, and handguns in the store and I have to know how they work, how to demonstrate them."

"Target shooting?"

Matt nodded. "We got a little space out back where we fire into a dirt bank."

"How far?"

Matt thought about it. "Ten, twelve yards, I guess."

Tom made a snort. "Can you hit what you aim at?

"Some of the time. Never seemed that important." He paused, then explained. "The customer always did most of the shooting."

"You got a handgun with you?" Patterson asked.

Matt nodded, rising. "In my saddle pack. I'll get it," he said. After a minute, he was back with a belt and a holstered revolver. He drew the Colt .38 from the holster and offered it for Tom's inspection. "Latest thing," he announced with pride. "Colt Lightning."

Tom took the revolver from him, checked to see if it was unloaded, then examined it. With a gesture of disdain, he laid it to one side on the table. "Too light and damned double action at that," he said with gruff scorn. "Can't trust 'em."

Matt took the contempt to heart. "They're the newest design," he protested. "We're selling a lot of them."

"Glad to hear it!" Tom said, rising to reach for a gun

belt with two revolvers on a peg by the door, sliding a
single-action Colt Peacemaker from one of the holsters
and holding it up with satisfaction. "And when one of
'em hangs up when it counts, this 'un will do the job."
He replaced the gun in its holster and fixed his eyes
upon Matt, his manner intent. "Look here," he said in
a solemn voice. "Let's get this straight about Jack
Moss." He paused, reflecting. "As I recall, Jack didn't
have a hell of a lot of good qualities. Mean, he was. I
think he done his share of backshooting, but, still, he
did fancy himself a gunfighter. Liked to think of himself as a Hickok or a Bill Longley. That is, when he was
damned sure that he was a lot faster than the fella he
faced."

Matt nodded. "Meaning someone like me."

Tom shrugged. "Ain't no way of telling. He might
call you out and, then again, he just might get you in his
rifle sights and do it that way." He shook his head. "I
don't know that I'm doing right by you or your pa doing
this thing." He drew a deep breath. "I been thinking on
it and it'd still be best if, maybe, I take Jack out instead
of you."

Instantly, Matt shook his head. "No, sir! My dad
wouldn't have it and neither would I," he said sternly.
"Dad said yesterday that we won't hire a killing."

Tom gave him a tight smile and cocked his head.
"Well, then, as I recall, you did have another idea," he
countered. "Something about getting outta the territory.
Now, that'd make a lot of sense."

"Dad would consider it running."

"What would you consider it?"

For a moment, Matt didn't reply. "Running," he said.

Tom sighed and took down the revolver again and absently twirled the cylinder. "Then, best you know that I ain't at all sure I can be of much help."

"You've made that clear," Matt responded, his solemnity matching Patterson's.

Betty came out of the bedroom wearing a gray dress and a little hat. "I'm going back to town, Tom," she announced. "Would you hitch up the buggy for me?"

"Ah, hell, Betty," Tom swore. "There's no need of that."

"Yes, there is," she argued determinedly. "You got to keep your mind on what Matt's pa paid you to do and there's no reason for me to stay out here and bother the two of you."

Matt rose from his seat, mystified. "Why, Mrs. Patterson," he said in confusion, "If I'm in the way—"

"Matt, boy," she cut in with gentle humor, "You ain't putting me out. Tom and I ain't married."

The young man's astonishment provoked laughter from the pair.

"I'd appreciate it, Tom," Betty said with a chuckle, "if you'd see me down to town."

"Hell," Tom swore, his laughter turning into a grumble, "if I can't talk you outta going, I'd be damned sure to see you right up to the front door of the Gold Strike." Seeing Matt's confusion, he added, "That's the saloon where Betty works."

"That'd be mighty nice of you, Tom," the young woman said matter-of-factly, accepting the offer as something due. "It's time that I was getting back anyhow."

"I now got me a bunch of money, Betty," Tom said plaintively. "You could stay fer quite awhile."

"Thank you kindly," she responded with a shake of her head. "That's sweet of you, Tom, but you'd best hold onto that money." She tiptoed to kiss him on the cheek. "You can come see me anytime and, maybe, after you all get acquainted, I might come out and spend a few days again."

Stepping away, she gestured to the side door. "Maybe we should leave while we've got the morning cool."

For a moment, Tom seemed inclined to argue. Then, with a stretch to show what a trouble it was, he walked slowly to the side door. "Come on," he said over his shoulder. "Give me a hand." He pointed at Matt's handgun on the table. "You might as well bring your plaything."

Obediently, Matt picked up the Colt, stuck it in the holster and followed him out the door, looking back at the attractive woman who returned his stare with a look of amused understanding.

Outside, he hurried to catch up with Tom who was striding toward the barn and strapping his gun belt around his waist. Matt, as well, buckled his belt and fell in step with Patterson. They walked in silence across the dry stubble yard and into the barn, then paused to let their eyes adjust to the shadows. There were four stalls, two on the left where Tom's horses were penned, two on the right with Matt's roan in the first, a chestnut mare in the next enclosure. Tom led the way to the mare, lifted the bar across the entrance and entered the stall. He reaching for a rope halter, slipped it over the mare's head, then led the horse to the center aisle of the barn where a two-seated open buggy was stored. "This is Betty's horse and rig. Hook 'er up," he instructed Matt. "I'll saddle our horses."

"You want me to go into Gold Stream with you?"

"Hate to leave you here all by yourself," Tom replied. "Jack Moss might've already got on your trail."

"Not likely," Matt responded. "I'll stay here and take the chance."

"No, you won't neither," Tom told him severely. "I aim to give your pa his money's worth and I ain't going to let you outta my sight till I got some idea that you can fend for yourself."

"Do you think that will ever happen?" Matt asked sarcastically as he struggled the mare between the traces.

"I told your pa that I'd do my best," Tom assured him. "Jes' come on along and enjoy the company."

For a few minutes more, they worked without speaking. Tom saddled his own chestnut gelding and the roan while Matt harnessed the mare to the rig. As Matt led the mare out into the sunlight, he turned to direct a low-voiced question: "Mr. Patterson, I don't mean to be impolite, but . . ." He cast a worried look at the house. "What is Miss Betty's full name?"

Tom squinted as he led the two horses out of the barn. "Damned if I know," he admitted with a short laugh. "Jes' always been Miss Betty to me."

"She works at the saloon?" Matt asked in some consternation. "Do you mean . . ."

"She's kinda like a waitress," Tom cut in hastily. "Jes' helps the house to keep the customers in a pleasant mood and urge 'em to spend a little more money than they'd ordinarily do." He nodded to indicate Betty as she came out of the house. "She don't work the rooms above the bar less she's a mind to."

Betty came toward them swiftly, extending her hand to Matt who, awkwardly, assisted her into the buggy.

"I'll hitch yours to the buggy," Tom told him as he tied the roan's reins to the rear of the platform. "You sit up there with Miss Betty and keep a tight rein on that mare."

Chapter Four

The three-mile trail to Gold Stream was not a road at all, but more a random path that meandered across the meadow to the downslope. Then, it snaked down the steep pass alongside a stream where men stood in the icy eddies to pan or work their rockers and long sluices for placer gold. Gold mining in Colorado had flourished for a while during and after the big rush in 1858 and 1959, but frustrations had been more prevalent than fortunes. The gold of the mountains had given birth to mining towns such as Idaho Springs, Cripple Creek and Golden, but some areas of the Rockies seemed more to tantalize the prospectors rather than to reward them. This high country location, miles away from Denver, had shown a few glittering successes over the years, but many more disappointments and failures. Still, every so often, hopefuls surged to the mountains at the news of a significant strike, however most eventually left with their dreams of riches unfulfilled. Only a few stubbornly remained to continue their hard-work searches in the streams and rock wall tunnels. Late in 1875, a sizable pocket of gold had been hacked out of the mountains and silver veins had been discovered as well. The mining camp of Gold Stream had been booming once again for over a year.

There had been little said between Matt and Betty on level ground and, as he guided the mare over the unfamiliar and precarious ground, there was no time for talk. On more than one occasion, the buggy tilted precariously, threatening to overturn. Each time, Betty was either thrown against or clutched herself to him for security, the soft feel of her body both an embarrassment and a pleasant experience. Each time, he'd glanced back at Tom trailing them on horseback, fearing Tom's displeasure at his close contact with the woman. He was surprised that the older man was paying scant attention to them. Most times his gaze was fixed far ahead, his sweeping glances examining the steep slopes on either side. From time to time, they could see men at their hard rock mining on the canyon walls, moving in and out of the dark holes of their claims.

In their descent, they forded the same stream twice, each time the buggy almost hub deep, the rush of the cascading water shuddering against the carriage. Matt clucked and used the whip to urge the mare to pull to the other bank. Then, as they came around a grove of aspen, the grade eased and Matt sat back with a little sigh of relief.

"Ain't that a sonofabitch?" Betty exclaimed.

Unaccustomed to such language from a woman, Matt merely nodded.

"It ain't no road at all," she informed him. "Only goes up to Tom's place and another old house over at the far end of the meadow. Nobody lives there anymore. Most times, 'less I go visit, he's up there all by himself summer and winter."

"Sounds lonely," Matt ventured. "Is he that sort of a man?"

"Has to be, I 'spect. Tried staying in town for a while, but they wouldn't leave him alone."

Matt looked at her. "Who?"

"All kinds of people," she replied. "People wanting to look at him, them that wanted to say that they'd had a beer with him, people who were wanting him to do foolish things for them—" She stopped suddenly.

"Like me and my pa?" Matt offered, his smile showing he wasn't offended.

"People wanting to find out if he was still handy with a gun," she resumed, a troubled look on her face. She gave him a glance. "You know who I mean?"

Matt considered the question and glanced back over his shoulder at the man on horseback. "Gunfighters?"

She nodded, a look of contempt coming into her face. "Little pissants, most of 'em. Thinking that he's getting too old to give 'em a fight, wanting to use his reputation to boost their own." She made a face.

"Do you mind if I ask something?"

"Depends," she answered. "Won't know till I hear it."

"He's got a ranch," Matt began uneasily, "but I don't see any livestock."

She gave him an easy grin. "You're asking if he still hires out his gun, is that it?"

Matt shrugged.

"Had a few beeves a couple of years ago, but they's more trouble than they was worth," she said. "Ever now and then, Tom and a couple of other fellers take a turn at this and that. Catching and breaking wild horses and selling for what they can." She paused, then continued, "One way or another, he gets by. I don't know that he's hired out his gun lately, but I guess he'd not likely tell me if he had." She watched Matt steadily for several moments. "You might ask him, maybe he'll tell you."

They rode on in silence, then moved out of trees into a mountain vale. Some distance ahead of them, the town of Gold Stream came into sight as a string of log and clapboard structures on either side of a dusty lane. Most of the commercial buildings were relatively new, only two showed the weathering of time. Plank sidewalks had been placed in front of the buildings on either side of the main street, useful when snow or rain would turn the thoroughfare into a slough. There were a few cabins and small tents fanned out behind the trade buildings and, at each end of the permanent structures, a scattering of larger tents had been erected.

"Town's been growing ever since they hit pay dirt again," Betty said. "Gonna be a real one someday soon. There's going to be a company mine, I hear."

"Those that come looking for Tom," Matt said, returning to that subject, "what's he do about them?"

"Avoids 'em if he can," she answered.

"What if he can't?" Matt persisted.

"He has his ways," she said noncommittally. She leaned forward and pointed. "You can stop there," she instructed. "I'll take it on to the livery from here."

Perplexed, Matt pulled up to halt the buggy. "We can take you the rest of the way, Miss—"

"I'll go on from here," she repeated and took the reins from his hands, nodding for Matt to step down.

She waited while he untied the roan, then snapped the reins with a cry, startling the mare forward at a brisk trot. She raised her hand in a farewell. "Happy to have made your acquaintance!" she called.

Matt turned an inquiring face to Tom as he rode up.

"Keeps her a little pride," Tom explained, his eyes following the diminishing buggy. "She don't like being seen leaving with a man or comin' back with one."

"Don't people know?" Matt asked, trying to keep the skeptical tone out of his voice.

"Why, sure they know," Tom answered. "But they act like they don't." He leaned over the pommel. "Leastwise, they'd better." He gestured to the roan. "We might as well ride in. Thanks to your pa, we can afford some salt pork, canned milk, bacon, flour and lard, and I'm plumb outta coffee. Gonna need some practice ammunition as well. You said you'd like to pick up some extra clothes, didn't you?"

Matt nodded and swung up on his horse.

"Gold Stream was jes' a few shacks and a couple of stores four years ago," Tom told him as they rode toward the town. "Back in '59, everybody thought these hills were just plumb full of gold. Some still do." He paused. "Now, there's a silver mining company fixing to set up here pretty soon."

"That's what Betty told me." He paused. "Silver?"

"Guess they'll have to rename the place," Tom mused. "Gold's probably pretty well played out around here, but they found some silver veins." He nodded his head. "That'll mean steady wages. Probably a good thing. It'll make it something other than just a squatting spot fer good-for-nothings. Maybe even into a real town."

"Would that be to your liking?" Matt asked.

Tom looked surprised. "Well, sure. I ain't no hermit even if I do live like one."

"Betty said you lived up there to stay away from people."

"Not all people," Tom corrected him. "Jes' strangers." He spurred his horse into a trot and, in kind, Matt followed. "I come to town pretty regular to visit with folks I know."

"You get snowed-in during the winter?"

Tom nodded. "Lordy, yes, sometimes. Although after a few days, I can usually pick my way down." They rode on for a few minutes. "It is my place, you know," he offered. "Your pa asked, but I wasn't a mind to tell him."

"Wasn't 'any of his business,' " Matt quoted.

Tom grinned. "Bought it from a young fella and his wife who'd come out here from Ohio. They'd built it, planning on ranching, hoping it to be their home fer the rest of their lives." He shook his head. "Couldn't stand the cold and the lonesome living. They was anxious to leave. I only paid five hundred dollars for it, half down and promised the rest some day if and when I ever hear from 'em again." He reflected on this. "They might be in Denver, but, then again, they might've turned around and gone back east."

They reached the first of the tents and rode toward the center of the boomtown. Most of the business shelters were marked with hand-lettered signs, some more legible than others, some even correctly spelled. The wooden buildings included a boardinghouse, an assay–office general store, a gunsmith's shop, a restaurant, a mining supply store, a barbershop, a freight office, a lean-to blacksmith's shop and a livery stable next to a lumberyard.

In the center of the mining town, a newer building stood out from the rest. A large and impressive structure, it was the only clapboard construction in town with a fresh coat of paint. The sign over the entrance to this great white building was a professional job, declaring it to be the Gold Strike Saloon. The windows, too, were painted and carried expertly lettered advertisements of good whiskey, superior entertainment, and honest gambling.

When Matt and his father had ridden through very early the day before, the town hadn't quite awakened, very few establishments having opened for business. Now, the mining town was bustling; a majority of men and a scant number of women were heading for various destinations on the plank walks. Although there were fewer men than in most mining camps, this one included blacks, Chinese, and an occasional Indian. After a dozen years since Lee's surrender, some ragged jackets, battered caps, and other remnants of both Union and Confederate uniforms could still be seen, the wearers living in close proximity with few signs of retained hostility.

With the canvas flaps up on either side, Matt could see that two of the large tents were combined fresh air saloons and gaming establishments. Rough slab bars and crude tables were moderately active; a surprising patronage in the early part of the day. Other tents included a long table eatery, a brothel, a laundry, a hell-and-damnation church and a big canvas enclosure that rented cots for the night.

Tom rode ahead, heading toward a large frame building, a long, gray, plain-faced structure with a crudely painted sign, *GOLD STREAM MERCANTILE*, across the boards over the two front windows. They rode to the hitching rail, tied their horses and walked in the open door.

Sunshine beamed through the door and the narrow windows, dust motes swirling lazily in the bright light. There were leather goods on the left side of a central aisle with saddles, bridles, whips, and harnesses. Across the aisle, near one window, ready-to-wear clothing was displayed on two dressmaker dummies. A man's alpaca suit, faded now, had stood too long in the harsh Colorado sun. A woman's dress with a low-cut bodice looked fresh and new, intended for a fancy lady, not a proper one.

From the gloom of the rear of the store, a cheerful voice called out, "Good morning to you, Tom!"

Matt took a step into the shadows, squinting, trying to adjust his eyes to the dim light. He could see only the movement of a figure in the central aisle, a massive shape lumbering toward them, blocking the light of the open door at the other end of the building. Then, the near giant emerged from the shadows, an immense man in the largest overalls Matt had ever seen, a broad smile slashing through the heavy beard on the ponderous head. "It's good to see you again!" The huge man's gaze flashed from Tom to Matt, his sharp eyes regarding Matt with interest.

"Morning to you, Nate," Tom responded, nodding to his companion. "Nathan Wainscote, meet Matt McKay. Staying with me for a while."

The big man reached out to Matt, his handshake revealing strength yet a surprisingly gentle grip. "Pleased to meet you."

"Thank you," Matt responded politely. "Myself as well."

"How high's my tally, Nate?" Tom asked.

"Not so high," the big man replied amiably.

"I'll settle her up and buy a few things I'll be needing," Tom told him. "Matt, here, he'll be looking for some work clothes." He paused, then added, "He'll be paying for those hisself."

"Right over there." Wainscote gestured to some rough shelves on the wall stocked with bolts of cloth, folded cotton shirts, and denim trousers. "There's a curtain over there where you can try 'em on."

Matt nodded and moved toward the area, wending his way through stacks of mining tools and equipment, past shovels, crowbars, picks, and lanterns.

Tom accompanied Wainscote to the back of the store where the hulking storekeep moved behind a crude plank counter to a battered roll-top desk in a makeshift office. He took a ledger book from a desk drawer and opened it, ran a sizable finger down a list of names and found the appropriate entry. "Twenty-nine, ninety-two," he told Tom.

"Need some salt pork, coffee . . . I got a list." Tom

unfolded a piece of paper and laid it on the counter. "And I'll need ten boxes of .45 caliber to take with me."

"Anything else?" Nate asked, scanning the list.

"Could use some beefsteaks, but maybe not this trip. As far as anything else, I still got some stuff down in the cellar."

The big man nodded, reached up to a shelf for a can of coffee, which he placed on the counter, then continued to fill the order.

"These will do," Matt said as he joined Tom at the counter, bringing two pairs of work pants and a couple of shirts.

Tom pointed to the clothing. "Didja try 'em on?"

Matt shook his head. "No need," he replied. "They're my size."

"You got more faith in store goods than I do," Tom said. "I 'spect you know what you're doing seeing as how you're in that line of work." He stared at Matt's bowler. "Ain't you gonna get yourself a new hat?"

Matt cocked his bowler to a jaunty position, then grinned. "Nope," he said. "This one fits me just fine."

Tom rolled his eyes, then gave a look to Wainscote who merely smiled.

Matt paid for his purchases, then watched as Tom took folded money from his pocket and carefully laid several bills on the counter.

"Okay, Tom," Wainscote sighed and gestured to the money on the counter. "That'll more than cover past due and what you got here." He reached to a different shelf behind him and started transferring ammunition boxes to the counter. "Hire out for a range war?"

Tom chuckled, but gave him no answer. "Here," Tom

said, turning to Matt, relaying the boxes. "Take these out and put 'em in our saddlebags. I'll bring the rest."

Matt said good-bye as Tom picked up the remaining packages and tipped his hat to Wainscote as they left.

Chapter Five

"Back to your place?" Matt asked as they finished loading the saddlebags.

"We got time for a drink or two," Tom told him and nodded to the Gold Strike Saloon down the street.

Matt looked at Patterson, then glanced up at the sun.

"I'll allow that it's a bit early," Tom said, catching the look.

"It's not even eleven," Matt exclaimed.

"It's a thing I do when I come to town," Tom declared. "Come on."

"I don't drink," Matt said.

"Well, then, you can watch me," Tom said. "'Less you want to sit over there in the shade till I come out."

"When'll that be?"

"Maybe an hour, maybe two. Whenever I damned well take the notion," Tom said peevishly.

Matt considered for a moment. "I'll ride back to the ranch. I'll see you there."

"You'll do no such thing," Tom countered. "Your pa put you under my protection and I'll want you where I can watch out fer you."

"He paid you to teach me to shoot," Matt corrected him, "not to nursemaid me."

"I'll be . . . only a half-hour," Tom said, changing his manner, his gaze shifting to the Gold Strike. "No more, I promise."

Matt waited for a moment, then shrugged.

They walked down the plank walk and pushed through the café doors into the saloon.

It was, by far, the finest and most impressive building in the otherwise shantytown. Even in the pale light of midday with the lantern chandeliers hanging cold and dark, there was a quiet resplendence to the saloon. The big main room was dominated by a long, ornately carved and highly polished walnut bar with a huge painting of a reclining, nearly nude woman centered on the wall behind it. In the large open room, there was a scattering of morning customers at the solid oak tables spaced across the smooth, pegged plank floor. At one special area of the room, there were carpets on the floor and green felt gaming tables. Two men in suits— gamblers from the looks of them—sat in casual conversation in this area.

"Good morning, Tom," the white-haired bartender greeted him with more civility than warmth. He nodded to Matt politely, his questioning eyes shifting to Tom.

"Matt McKay," Tom supplied the name, a cock of his head toward his companion. "Meet J. C. Farley, best barkeep this side of San Francisco."

J. C. Farley nodded again to Matt, but didn't extend his hand.

"We'll take a bottle of your best Kentucky mash," Tom said. "And you might put a couple more aside fer when we leave."

The bartender lifted an eyebrow at the order, but didn't move to fill it.

Instantly vexed, Tom reached into his pocket and unfolded a couple of bills from the thick pad of money. "Whatever that'll buy, J. C."

Still, the bartender didn't move.

"It'll be all right, J. C.," came a strong voice.

Tom and Matt both turned, following the bartender's glance.

A portly, distinguished man, sixty if a day, was coming down the stairway from the upper floor. As if to belie his age, his movements were smooth and languid, a hint of quickness in his step, a sense of strength in the jeweled hand that glided along the banister.

"If you say so, Mr. Calvecci," the bartender said dutifully, sweeping the money out of sight, placing a bottle of Kentucky sour mash on the counter, two small glasses beside it. "Water, Tom?"

Tom lifted a hand in a negative gesture.

"Good morning, Tom," Calvecci said. He turned to Matt, appraising him with a sweeping glance, then extended his hand. "I'm Joseph Calvecci," he introduced himself, indicating the saloon with a turn of his silvered head. "Welcome to my place."

Matt took the hand awkwardly. "Matthew McKay. You have a very nice establishment."

"Friend or family?" the man asked in a cheerful manner, a nod to indicate Tom.

"We . . . have business," Matt explained lamely.

For a fleeting moment, a slight frown tugged at the corners of the proprietor's mouth and then it was gone as he turned to Tom. "No trouble this time, Tom."

"I don't plan on it, Joe," Tom replied.

"It finds you nonetheless," Calvecci countered with an almost sympathetic tone of voice.

Tom arched his eyebrows, making no comment.

The saloon owner gave him a tight smile, then moved away toward the gamblers at the far end of the saloon.

Tom picked up the bottle and the glasses from the bar and carried them to a nearby table. He pulled out a chair for himself and motioned to one for Matt. "Sit awhile," he said. He poured a drink for Matt and filled his own glass.

Matt pushed his glass away.

"Had a bit of a scrape last time I was in," Tom said, gesturing to the bar, then sipped his whiskey.

Matt responded with a questioning expression.

"I got to showing off and put a couple of bullet holes in his fancy bar, I did," Tom confessed. "Had old J. C. ducking fer cover which has, I guess, still got him peeved." He peered at the bar. "Can't see that I did 'er any harm." He finished the drink in a gulp and poured another. "Joe thinks a heap of ever'thing he's got in this place."

"Can't blame him," Matt remarked, looking around. "Does he do much business? Enough to afford all this?"

"Hard to say," Tom mused. "Wouldn't think so, not

with a couple of them other tent saloons undercutting him. 'Course, they serve pretty raw liquor and they ain't got the best looking girls." He poured and finished a second round. "I guess he's figgering that Gold Stream's gonna be an up-and-comer someday."

"You said there was a mining company coming in," Matt reminded him.

"That's the talk," Tom said with a nod, reaching for Matt's glass. "Sure you ain't gonna have a drink with me?"

Matt shook his head. "Never got a taste for it," he said, half in apology.

Tom raised the glass to his lips with a steady hand. He paused, his eyes locking with Matt's, a look of near-defiance that somehow softened into regret. "It ain't necessarily a thing to apologize for, boy. A man really ought to have better sense." Nonetheless, he tossed the whiskey down in one gulp, scarcely wincing at the sting.

Tom sat in silence for a period of time, putting down four more shots in rapid order before settling into a more languid manner of drinking. Without any seeming effect, he had half-emptied the bottle in less than twenty minutes.

"Aren't we about ready?" Matt asked.

"A little longer," Tom responded, pouring still another. "Just a couple more and we'll be on our way."

As noonday came and passed into late afternoon, business picked up in the Gold Strike. The room was nearly full now; miners, drifters and ranch hands at the tables and crowded at the bar. J. C. Farley had another bartender helping him pour drinks and, circulating through the tables, three women in fancy dresses flirted with the men. There were two card games going on in the back of the saloon and, watching it all from an elevated chair in a corner, Joseph Calvecci smoked a cigar in apparent contentment.

Two men walked by their table, both of them smiling with scorn at the sight of Tom Patterson now facedown on the table.

"Goddamned drunk," one said. "Calvecci ought to shag his tail outta here."

"Don't let him hear you," the other man said with mock caution. "He's d-a-a-a-ngerous." They both laughed and pushed past to join friends at a nearby table.

The swinging doors of the saloon slapped opened and a burly man stepped inside, a glint of a badge barely visible beneath his vest. He wore a gun on his hip and carried a polished, hickory baton at waist-level in his right hand. He was of some indeterminate middle age, beefy, but there was muscle as well. He swaggered with a bearing of intimidating strength and intensity. Under a balding pate, he wore a brooding face with an unvarying expression of distrust and suspicion. His eyes swept across the barroom, an oppressor looking for troublemakers and somewhat disappointed not to find one. Then, his eyes settled on Tom and his expression changed to something close to hatred. His gaze shifted to Matt and a questioning look appeared. He stared at the two of them for a few moments, then gave an abrupt, beckoning motion to Matt as he moved to a table and laid the hickory club upon it.

"Me?" Matt mouthed the word with some uncertainty.

The big man scowled. "Get over here!" he said loudly, bringing attention to himself and to Matt. He sat down heavily and, again, gave a contemptuous, summoning sweep of his hand to Matt.

Aware of the curious eyes upon him, Matt took his time to scrape back his chair and walk across the room to the table, trying not to look too submissive or foolish.

"Sit down," the man commanded as he pointed to a chair. "Dutch Snyder," he announced. "I'm town marshal."

Matt remained standing. "Matthew McKay. From Nebraska City. What's this about?"

Snyder regarded him closely, somewhat surprised at Matt's firm manner. "I like to know who's in town and what their business might be," he said brusquely. "I don't know who Mr. Matthew McKay from Nebraska City might be, but I reckon I can usually tell something about a man by the riffraff he runs with."

Matt didn't respond immediately, taking careful measure of the man. "We're respectable enough people in our community, Mr. Synder," Matt said evenly. "If you think it's worth the trouble, you can check me out."

"I ain't got time for that," Snyder complained gruffly, nodding his head at Patterson. "What are you doing with that barfly?"

The situation was embarrassing. The men and women in the barroom murmured.

Matt decided to be direct. "With all due respect, Mr. Snyder, that's my business and none of your affair."

"That's *Marshal* Snyder . . . and everything that goes on in my town is my affair," Snyder said as he reached to grasp his formidable club. "You sass me one more time, boy, and I'll take your teeth out."

Neither of them had noticed Joseph Calvecci until he glided into a chair at the table. "Good afternoon, Dutch," he said in a light, cordial tone that did not veil a firm voice. "What brings you to see us today?"

"Making my rounds," Snyder replied curtly, irritated at what he considered an intrusion.

"I wasn't aware that the Gold Strike was of concern to you," Calvecci countered. "We're not really a part of your, ah, protective arrangement."

"Naw, you sure ain't," Snyder responded. "You sure don't pay your share for me keeping the peace."

"We run a nice, quiet place," Calvecci assured him. "And we take care of our own troubles."

Snyder jerked his head toward the insensible Tom Patterson. "Like him shooting up the place a few weeks ago? Damned drunk could've killed somebody!"

"Drunk or sober, Tom Patterson would never kill anybody by accident," Calvecci declared. "And, if I were you, I wouldn't be quite so loud in your opinion. He might hear it."

Anger flushed the big man's face, his jaw muscles tightening yet he made no move toward the older man, showing a hesitancy under the cold, steady gaze of the saloon proprietor. "You watch how you talk to me, wop," he blustered. He jerked his head toward the prostrate Patterson. "I know you call him 'stead of me at times, but there ain't nobody worried about him and his reputation no more. He ain't nothing but a falling-down drunk. I gotta mind to drag him outta here down to the jail."

Calvecci kept his smile in place even though the

pitch of his voice gave a hint of derision. "Just hope that he wouldn't wake up along the way."

Snyder sat speechless for a few seconds and then, awkwardly, he turned his attention to Matt again. "What's your business with Patterson? Hiring his gun?"

Matt hesitated. "Just visiting. I'm . . . a friend."

Snyder gave a cough of disbelief. "Friend?" he scoffed. "That's a lie and you know it. Tom Patterson ain't got a friend in the world."

"There's nothing against the law about visiting," Matt responded. "Nothing at all."

Snyder looked from Matt to Calvecci, then heaved himself up, swinging the baton carelessly, dangerously. "Well, *friend*, you get your pal up and outta here. I don't want to see either one of you in town again."

An angry response rose in Matt's throat, but Calvecci intervened quickly. "We'll take care of it, *Marshal*," he said emphasizing the title with some mockery. "You have my word on it."

"Now, what's that worth?" Snyder said scathingly. He raised the heavy rod and jabbed it into Matt's chest for emphasis. "If there's a next time, I'll make you sorry."

Without another word, he turned and walked away, strutting through the saloon doors.

Matt stared after him. "Is he really the law?" he asked in disbelief.

"No, not at all," the saloon owner replied with scorn. "A bully of a man who came to town a few months ago and set himself up as some sort of a lawman. Talked or browbeat some of the locals into paying him to keep order."

"Then . . . he's not official?"

Calvecci gave a quick smile and a chuckle. "Nothing's quite official in Gold Stream, Matt. Oh, we do have a government of sorts . . . a mining camp council."

Matt raised an eyebrow in question.

"The miners, merchants, and others here get together from time to time and vote on people from their groups to represent them," Calvecci explained. "Gold Stream is nothing but a mining camp right now. We don't usually have a lot of problems, but the council is supposed to be there to work out the ones we have. Claim procedures, community concerns, keeping the peace when need be—"

"Where's Snyder fit in?" Matt interrupted.

"That's just the point," Calvecci replied. "It's the council's job to appoint a peace officer." He shook his head. "This is a sorry lot this time around, not a decent brain between any two of them. I blame them more than Snyder. He came to town, declared himself the town marshal and they've done nothing to disclaim him."

"Why not?" Matt asked incredulously.

"Can't be bothered," Calvecci said regretfully. "Too busy with their own affairs to realize what they've let into town." He sighed, then nodded at the doorway, indicating the departed Snyder. "I'm not saying that we don't need somebody here to handle the hooligans, but we need to appoint a good man, a fair man. Trouble with Dutch is that he's tough on those who are weak and on happy drunks, but he's nowhere to be found if there's real trouble. Council ought to do their job and tell Snyder to head on down the road. If they don't . . ." He left the rest unspoken.

Matt looked toward Tom Patterson. "What was that about you calling for Tom?"

"Only on a couple of occasions," Calvecci said with a nod. "Only when we get someone that we can't handle. No matter what Dutch says, when Tom's sober and steady, he's not one you want to challenge." He gave Matt a shrug of apology and walked away, heading back toward his elevated chair.

Matt took Tom by the arm to shake him awake. "Come on, Mr. Patterson," he said firmly. "It's getting late. We gotta get on home."

"Just leave him be, Matt," Betty said from behind him. Matt turned around and blinked his surprise at her appearance. The woman he'd escorted into town had transformed; her face was rouged, her hair swept up into a bun, a rose-hued silk dress cut tight against her upper torso and flaring at the hips, the bodice low and revealing.

"My working clothes," she acknowledged, taking a step away to show off the gown. "Ordered in special from St. Louis."

"You're . . . pretty, Miss Betty," he said in embarrassment, then turned away with a gesture to Tom sprawled across the table. "What do I do about him?"

Betty shook her head, dismayed. "He promised," she sighed, mostly to herself. "I guess he can't help it."

"Miss Betty . . ." Matt hesitated, not sure that he should continue. "Did you see . . . ?"

She nodded wearily. "Yes, Matt." A touch of bitterness came into her voice. "Snyder wouldn't dare to brace Tom if he was sober." She stepped closer to the senseless man, reaching her hand out to touch him, almost as a caress. "Can you find your way back to the ranch?"

Matt nodded. "Sure, I suppose. What about him?"

"I'll see to him," she said, a gesture of her head summoning the bartender. "You get on. He'll be there tomorrow."

"What about Snyder?" Matt asked.

"We won't worry about him, he's mostly just talk," she told him.

Matt rose from his chair uncertainly, stepping back to watch as J. C. Farley came around the end of the bar, touched a husky customer on the shoulder and motioned for him to follow. They stepped to either side of Tom Patterson and lifted him between them. To the amusement of the crowd, they carried him up the stairway, then out of sight.

"Seems like they've seen that before," Matt said, feeling angry.

"Mad at them or him?" Betty asked.

"Him, mainly," Matt shot back, "for letting it happen." He paused, his mind working, his expression showing it. "I think I'll get an early start for Nebraska City in the morning."

Betty stared at him. "Go home to get killed?" she asked with disdain. "Is that what you want to do?

"What's my option? Rely on a drunk to keep me alive? A lot of help he'll be."

Anger flashed in the young woman's eyes. "He may be a lot of things, honey, but he's a man of his word. He made a bargain with your pa and he'll do what he's been paid to do. Or, at least, he'll try his very best." She gave a curt nod toward the stairway. "I'll take care of Tom. Now, by God, you git yourself back to the ranch."

Matt didn't move, surprised at the young woman's intensity.

"You heard me!" she said in a low voice. "Now, git!"

"Yes, ma'am," he responded with an obedient nod. "What about his horse?"

"He'll be on it sometime tomorrow," she said in vexation. "You just worry about yourself."

With another nod, Matt turned and walked away.

Outside, with the day turning into evening, he transferred Tom's saddlebags onto his own horse. *Tom will probably think they've been stolen*, he mused and laughed about it. He mounted the roan and, with a glance at the long shadows of the evening sun, spurred the horse toward the mountain trail.

Chapter Six

Matt was up and out early the next morning to saddle his horse for a ride. He rode across the high meadow, a horseman unsure of himself and his mount. Nonetheless, there was a feeling of exhilaration as he rode, a sense of adventure as he explored the upper mesa. The sun was not yet high enough in the sky for warmth and the horse was frisky in the early day chill, hard to hold to a brisk canter. On occasion, almost fearfully, Matt let the horse have his head and, hanging on, found himself enjoying the gallop as well. Then, reluctantly, he reined in, unwilling to risk a fall for either himself or the horse on unfamiliar ground.

Scouting my surroundings, he told himself, knowing that his real reason was not to be at the ranch when Tom Patterson returned. It would not be a pleasant moment; Patterson's temper would surely be as nasty as his massive hangover.

He rode to the edge of the basin, then followed a trail that wound up in the surrounding mountains. He settled back and let the horse pick his way up the steep path. He enjoyed the view that became breathtakingly beautiful as they climbed higher. It was a magnificent vista, the sun now high in the azure sky illuminating the entire panorama, the air clean and clear without a trace of mist or summer haze. Later in the day, perhaps, the light might turn flat and drab, but, now, it was splendid, a perfect morning.

Below, he could see the ranch house, miniaturized by distance, and another dwelling at the far end of the meadow. From this far view, it looked a near ruin, barely standing.

The sun was at late morning when he turned the horse back down the trail. A few minutes later, from a switchback looking east, he saw a tiny horse and rider—Tom Patterson coming home. Matt watched from his elevated view as Tom got down wearily, tied his horse at the front of the house and moved inside. Matt sat a minute more, then turned the roan down the path, clucking softly to his animal.

Matt endured the jolting ride as his horse, by now eager to return to the stable, moved into a hard-to-restrain trot. When at last they arrived at the ranch house yard, Matt noted that Tom's horse was still at the hitching rail, looking a bit forlorn in the noonday sun. Matt dismounted and, with one hand on the roan's bridle, untied Tom's horse with the other. He led the pair of them toward the barn, took off their bridles and saddles, and rubbed them down, forking hay into each stall before walking to the house.

"I was gonna take care of the horse," Patterson said when Matt entered the main room.

It took a moment for Matt's eyes to adjust, to locate the man standing in a shadowed corner.

"How're you feeling?" Matt asked.

"All right, I guess," came the answer. Tom stepped out into the sunlight, almost ashen, the bright beam causing him to squint. "Make a fool of myself?"

Matt looked away without an answer.

"Guess I did," Tom muttered.

He stood for a few moments, then crossed over to the window and looked out. Abruptly, he turned to Matt. "Won't happen again. Not as long as you're here." He paused, peering at Matt. "You want your money back? At least, what I got left of it?"

Matt considered his answer. "I don't know."

"It's yours if you want it. If you want to call the deal off, I wouldn't blame you."

"I'd really rather get on with what I came for," Matt said, not hiding his annoyance. "If you're up to it."

The older man was silent for a short time, then nodded. "Gimme a couple of hours," he said huskily. "Then we'll start." Without a further word of explanation, Tom walked into his bedroom and shut the door.

In the late afternoon, they walked to what remained of a corral behind the ranch house. Tom carried a two-holster gun belt slung over his shoulder, a Colt revolver in each. As they came to the neglected enclosure, he motioned Matt to a standstill, stepped over the fallen rails, then walked across the paddock to the opposite side. He kicked the rails from either side of a post isolating it, then walked back toward Matt, his stride deliberate and measured, his lips moving as he counted.

He motioned for Matt to join him as he drew a line in the dirt with the toe of his boot and handed the gun belt to the young man as he came to the mark. "Here," he said. "Took these off a man down in Santa Fe. They got a good feel to 'em and they're true enough."

"Do I need two?" Matt asked doubtfully, reluctantly strapping the belt around his waist. "I'd look the fool."

"Most only carry one," Tom admitted. "I carry at least one extra, sometimes more. If one don't work, you sure as hell want a spare."

Matt drew the revolvers from their holsters several times, noticing the ease with which each came free. "Feels like he must've used them considerably." He looked at Tom. "Anybody famous?"

Tom shook his head. "Nobody you would've heard of," he said, adding cryptically, "Pretty well known in certain circles down around Texas and Mexico." He gestured to the post. "See if you can hit that."

Matt nodded, replaced the revolvers in the holsters and poised his hands above the guns, ready to draw.

"Ah, hell!" Patterson swore in exasperation. "Forget about the damned draw. Jes' take out one of them pistols and see if you can hit that post."

Feeling chastised, Matt pulled the revolver from the right holster and, squaring himself to the target, took aim.

"Nope, not that way," Tom said, stepping forward, his hands grasping Matt's shoulders, turning him sideways. "Don't give him so much of you to hit." He gave

Matt a grin and feinted a blow to the young man's groin. "Better to walk with a limp than get your pecker shot off." He nodded to the post. "Now, let 'er fly."

Matt raised the revolver once again and held it at arm's length, the position awkward to him. He jerked back the hammer and fired.

The boom of the shot echoed from the surrounding mountains, but there was no sound of the bullet hitting wood.

"Again."

Once more, Matt aimed, cocked, and fired.

For a second time, there was no impact at the post.

Tom reached for the gun. "Look here," he instructed. "Pull back the hammer, *then* aim." He handed the revolver back to Matt. "Try 'er now."

Matt nodded, bringing the handgun to a fully outstretched arm position, steadied it, cocked it, aimed and fired.

This time, the bullet ticked at the side of the post, about six inches from the top.

"Better," Tom said gruffly.

Matt pulled the hammer back, pulled the trigger and fired again, missing the post.

"Aim it carefully and *squeeze* the trigger this time."

Matt looked at him with some annoyance. "I squeezed it last time," he complained.

"Squeeze it easier, then," Tom said. "Try it."

Matt cocked the hammer, took time in his aim and gently squeezed the trigger.

"Good shot!" Tom exclaimed as the bullet slapped into the post.

Matt smiled at the compliment. "What's next?"

"Next?" Tom's voice was cutting. "You stand out here for the next couple of hours shooting at that post." He handed Matt two boxes of .45 cartridges. "Take your time between shots, don't waste 'em. And use both guns."

"You mean . . . at the same time?" Matt asked.

Tom looked pained. "Hell, no," he exclaimed. "Remember that the second gun is a spare. You're right-handed so you'd best shoot with your right." He started walking away.

"Where'll you be?" Matt asked in surprise.

"Right over there on the porch in the shade," Tom replied, pointing to the ranch house. "Maybe taking a little nap."

For an hour and a half, Matt stood in the heat of the intense sunlight, aiming and firing at the post. As instructed, he took his time and squeezed off each shot with studied deliberation. By the time he ran out of ammunition, he was hitting it on average of one out of four attempts.

"How'd I do?" he asked, coming onto the front porch as he wiped the sweat from his forehead with his sleeve.

"Not bad," Tom responded noncommittally, rocking his straight-backed chair to lean against the log wall.

"Should I continue?" Matt asked.

Tom shook his head. "Naw, that's enough for right now," he advised. "But I want you to come out first thing in the morning and go at it for a couple of hours, then a couple more hours in the afternoon."

"For how long?"

"Till you can hit that post every time," Tom responded.

"Damn!" Matt swore uncharacteristically. "I don't think I'll ever be able to do that."

Tom countered with a positive nod. "You'd better before you face Jack Moss." He motioned Matt toward the ranch house door. "We'll call 'er quits for the day. Any good at cooking?"

"I suppose so," Matt replied. "My dad and I've been taking turns at it since my mom died five years ago."

Tom nodded. "Hoping you could," he said. "Tired of my own. Be a welcome change. Wash up now and we'll have at 'er."

They worked together in the kitchen, Tom bringing in firewood while Matt rummaged through the closet pantry.

"Well, you're well enough supplied with beans," Matt called out in mild admonition. "Shouldn't have any problems with constipation."

"There ought to be some tinned meat in there some-wheres, maybe down in the cellar," Tom called back. "Although we probably ought to cook this salt pork we jes' brought home."

With a sigh, Matt took one of the cans of beans from the shelf and came out into the kitchen where the smoke from the salt pork was already rising from the skillet. "Thought you wanted me to cook?" Matt said questioningly.

"Hand me the can," Tom responded. "Don't figure there's many different ways of frying pork and beans."

*   *   *

After supper, they sat on the porch again and watched the light behind the western mountains fade into darkness. The heat of the day had disappeared and a light breeze bore the chill down from the snow-capped peaks.

"Too cool for you?" Tom asked, drawing on his pipe, the glow from the bowl faintly illuminating his face.

"No, feels good," Matt replied, shivering a bit nonetheless. "It's pretty, but it must get cold up here during the winter."

Tom nodded. "It's a right snug cabin in spite of what your old man thinks of it." He drew on the pipe again, making a sucking noise. "When a storm hits, I jes' hole up here and wait till she's over."

"Till spring?" Matt laughed.

"Sometimes it seems like that," Tom answered amiably.

"The other cabin across the meadow?" Matt questioned. "Who lived there?"

"Don't rightly know. It's been there quite awhile, some prospector I reckon. Some say that the Indians were a bother."

"You have any trouble with Indians?"

"Not so far. I see some Utes from time to time crossing the meadow. They keep their distance and I keep mine. See a few in Gold Stream once in a while, but they don't stay more than an hour or two."

"How'd you decide on this area? Weren't you down in the south? Texas and Arizona?" Matt asked, changing the subject.

"Didn't seem like such a good idea to hang around down there," Tom replied. "Too many people didn't much appreciate my line of work."

"Lawmen?"

"Some of that, some of the other. It didn't seem to matter which side I was on, I made some fellas mad at me."

"How did you learn to handle a gun—the war?"

Tom took his time, his prolonged silence indicating that he might not answer at all. Finally, he said, "Not really. Gave me some practice at the blue bellies, that's all."

They sat for a while, neither speaking, the darkness enveloping them. Finally, Tom cleared his throat. "I grew up in Texas. Don't have any folks to speak of. Don't remember my mother at all and, from what I hear, it wasn't no loss. My pa was nothing but trash, worked from town to town swamping bars to get enough to eat and drink . . . mostly drink." Tom shook his head. "I got away from him when I was no bigger than maybe seven or eight. On my own since then."

"How'd you live?"

"I'd been doing most of the work for my old man anyhow," Tom's voice was full of scorn. "Jes' kept on doing what folks wanted. Swept up floors, took out garbage, whatever they didn't want to do themselves. Sometimes, I'd get my butt beat if I didn't do something like they thought it ought to be done." He paused and his voice changed, softer. "Lots of folks that you wouldn't think it of did what they could fer me. Bartenders that'd fix me a meal and let me sleep in the storerooms, upstairs ladies that would buy me some clothes or give me some of what they earned."

Matt sat quietly, not wanting to interrupt.

"I saw a couple of gunfighters when I was a kid," Tom went on. "Folks busted their butts to take care of 'em, scared to death of 'em, let 'em have anything they wanted." He paused. "One of 'em made a big fuss over me, showing off now that I think back on it. He'd show me how fast he could draw, how good he was at hitting a target. I wanted to be like him . . . to have everybody look up to me."

"How old were you then?"

"Ten or eleven. I don't rightly know." He laughed. "Hell, I don't know exactly how old I am now! Nobody ever told me when I was born." He rose from his chair and began knocking out his pipe. "'Spect it's time to go to bed, for me, at least."

"Me too," Matt agreed, rising and moving toward the door.

"We might as well get it all said," Tom said bluntly, his tone of voice arresting Matt's attention. "Shot and killed my first man when I was fourteen. Killed two others and robbed a bank before I ever took to shaving regular." He paused, then continued, "Don't know that everybody I killed needed it, but most of 'em did. I ain't apologizing, you understand?"

"Not really," Matt responded. "Not even with what you've told me."

"What do you mean?"

"Those people who showed you kindness . . . why didn't you take after them?"

Without waiting for a reply, Matt opened the door and went inside.

Tom stood for a few moments. Then, he resumed his seat, refilling his pipe as he leaned back and looked up into the vast dome of a billion stars.

Chapter Seven

"Lame bunch, Bob."

"Well, I guess we make do with what we got, boss. Not like the old gang."

"Now, we got snot-nosed kids and old wannabes."

Jack Moss and Bob Daly sat side-by-side on the front steps of a cabin deep in the dense woods of the Missouri Ozarks. Moss was a tall man in his late thirties with a slender build, his face lean and lupine with a neatly trimmed beard. His companion was a husky, pug-faced man.

Twenty feet away in the weed-filled clearing, two men were wrestling while four others circled around them. There were shouts and cries of encouragement from the onlookers as the wrestlers circled, feinted, and grabbed at each other. The younger of the two lunged and caught his opponent's leg, heaved it up and tumbled him to the ground. The older man rolled to his knees in an attempt to rise, but the young man was quickly on him, his arm around his neck.

"Hey, Luke! You ain't gonna let him do that to ya!" yelled one man.

"Ride him, Jimmy!" cried another. "Break his damn neck!"

The older man, Luke, twisted away from the encircling arm, broke free and swung a fist into the midsection of his opponent. More surprised than hurt, the young man stepped back.

"No punching, Luke!" one of the onlookers proclaimed. "You're supposed to 'ressling, not fighting."

"Sonofabitch was choking me," Luke responded, now on his feet and circling, his arms rotating his clenched fists.

"Just funning ya, Luke," Jimmy said, backing away. "Don't get sore."

"Fun's over!" the older man said, swinging his right hand, angered anew as Jimmy stepped farther away.

"Want me to stop it, Jack?" Daly asked, half-rising from the steps.

"Sit down. Let 'em fight," Moss said.

Daly, Moss' second in command, resumed his seat, although his eyes remained on the escalating fight between the two outlaws. "Luke's getting mad. You know how he gets."

"Let 'em fight," Moss repeated. "What else they got to do? Been sitting around for days."

"They're fidgety, all right," Daly agreed. "I'm surprised we ain't had trouble among 'em before now."

"Hello to the cabin!" came a distant cry from the woods.

Both Moss and Daly came instantly to their feet, guns drawn. Alarmed, the men in the yard turned toward the dense forest, the wrestling match and resultant fight forgotten. After a few seconds, they scattered, running to pick up the guns and rifles they'd left near the cabin or on the porch.

"Who or what the hell is that?" Moss asked. "We expecting somebody?"

Daly shook his head.

A wagon-width break in the wall of elms, white pines, hickories and maples marked the only entrance into the clearance, but no one could be seen in that passageway.

"Permission to come in!" the voice sounded again.

"Show yourself!" Moss shouted. "What do you want here?"

"I'm a friend! Looking to join up!"

The man still couldn't be seen, he was hidden somewhere in the forest.

"If he don't come in, you and the boys see to it that he don't get out of these woods alive," Moss said to Daly, then raised his voice once again. "Show yourself right now or you're a dead man!"

"Don't shoot, fellers! Pete Tatum sent me." A gangly young man on a chestnut horse came out of the trees, hands held high above his head. "Told me you was looking fer some to ride with ya."

Under the barrels of considerable firepower, the young man spurred his horse forward with his hands still held high.

"Who are you?" Moss called.

"Jim Wilkins, Mr. Moss. That's who I'm addressing, ain't I?"

"Come on in," Moss commanded. "You boys shoot him if he does anything funny."

As the rider came into the yard, one of the gang reached for and took the revolver from his hip as he passed, then another took the rifle from his saddle holster.

"Can I get down?"

Moss nodded and walked forward as Wilkins dismounted, his handgun trained on the man's chest. "Pete sent you?" Moss said vehemently. "He told you where to find me?"

Wilkins nodded and made a sweeping gesture to the group surrounding him. "I'd appreciate it if you'd kinda keep them guns pointed down. I ain't armed now as you can see."

"See if he's got a hideout gun on him," Moss instructed. Daly moved quickly to run his hands over the man's jacket, shirt, jeans, and even inside his boots. "He's okay, Jack."

"Where's Pete?" Moss asked, annoyance in his voice. "I sure as hell don't like you coming here and just saying that Pete sent you. How do I know that's so? If that's a fact, why didn't he come with you?"

"He can't hardly stand on that one leg of his much less ride," Wilkins told him. "Damned fool fell off his horse last week, that's why. Dead drunk and let that damned nag dance all over him."

Moss regarded the young man closely for a few seconds, then nodded and waved to his men, dismissing them. "Since you're here, come on inside and let me find out a few things about you." With Daly following behind with his revolver still in hand, Moss led the newcomer onto the cabin porch and through the front door into the cabin.

There were two rooms in the cabin and bedrolls littered the earthen floors in each of them. There was a cookstove in one corner of the larger room and a table with four chairs. No other furniture occupied the cabin.

"Sit down," Moss told Wilkins, motioning him to one of the chairs at the table. As the new man seated himself, Moss took a chair across from him while Daly stood watchfully nearby.

"I come to join up," Wilkins said. "Heard you was needing men with experience."

"What experience would that be?" Moss asked.

"Well, I rode with the Reno brothers up in Indiana a few years back. You know Frank or Sim?"

"Know of 'em," Moss answered.

"Well, I was with 'em on a couple of saloon stickups. You heard about the Marshfield job?"

"The train thing? That was what, eight or nine years ago?"

Wilkins nodded. "Yeah, May of '68, the Adams Express job. I was in on that."

Moss studied the man for several seconds before speaking. "That was a mighty big deal. Must've got a lot of money outta that."

Again, Wilkins nodded. "It was a good one, you betcha. We stuck up the train about twenty miles south of Marshfield and got the safes in the express car. Papers said we got like a hundred thousand, but it waren't nothing near that big." He paused, rolled his eyes and waved his hand in a dismissive manner. "Whatever it was, some of us sure didn't get much. If you waren't one of the Reno brothers, they waren't likely to give you a big share."

"I understand they could be pretty mean about that sort of thing," Moss agreed. "That the reason you split with 'em?"

Wilkins shook his head. "I got along with 'em okay, but then I am a fella who don't complain a lot. Truth is, they just went their way and I went mine. That's all there was to it."

"You're a long way from Indiana," Daly interjected. "How do we know you really did ride with the Renos?"

Wilkins turned to Daly in a self-effacing manner. "I know that it pays fer you to be suspicious, but all I got is my word that it's the truth. You got any doubts, I'll ride on out and that'll be the end of it."

Moss and Daly exchanged a glance that Wilkins didn't miss. "That is, if you'll let me."

"You've been around a few years," Moss said. "You're what, thirty?"

"Just under. Thirty next birthday."

"Whatcha been doing recently?"

"Not a whole lot. Talked with the Youngers for a bit, but nothing came of it."

Moss took his time considering the situation, then finally nodded. "I do need men, I'll tell you that," Moss said, pointing to Daly. "Bob and me and a couple of others are what's left of my old bunch. New ones, like yourself, I don't know all that well. You afraid of getting killed? Or 'fraid of killing someone?"

"I ain't wanting to get killed if that's what you

mean," Wilkins answered. "Guess no one does, but if we're doing the job and the job's done right, I figger I'll be okay."

"How about the killing?"

"Don't do it unless I need to. Is that the right thing to say?"

Moss gave a slow nod. "All I want is a fella who ain't too skittish or too afraid on the job. I don't want a fella who starts shooting 'cause he ain't got any better sense. Likely he starts shooting, others start shooting back."

"I'm steady, Mr. Moss," Wilkins assured him. "Oh, by the way," Wilkins said suddenly, reaching inside his jacket, "I just now remembered. Pete sent along a letter. Letter fer you." He took a crumpled envelope from his jacket pocket and handed it across the table.

Moss scowled as he examined the envelope and started to open it. "Why didn't you say that right off?"

"Maybe I should've," Wilkins admitted. "All them guns pointing at me, I kinda forgot."

Moss took out the letter and unfolded it, scanning the signature at the bottom. "From my cousin, Will," he said as he began to read. For a short time, the room was silent, then Moss swore under his breath. "Jared, my kid brother. Some damned dry goods clerk over in Nebraska City shot and killed him."

For a couple of minutes, neither Wilkins nor Daly spoke. Then, Daly cleared his throat, "I'm real sorry, Jack. I knowed you doted on the boy."

"That sonofabitch! He shotgunned him, Bob!" Tears welled in the outlaw leader's eyes and he wiped his sleeve across his face.

"I'm sorry to bring you such bad news," Wilkins

muttered. "I didn't know what was in the letter, you know."

Moss rose from his chair and began to pace the room, his face flushed with anger. He strode the length of the room several times, staring straight ahead.

Daly and Wilkins sat very still, watching as their leader's fury continued to build.

Suddenly, he stopped and turned to Daly. "Get the boys ready to ride."

Daly stood in stunned silence for several seconds, then said, "What do you mean, boss?"

Moss began to pace again. "We're going to Nebraska City. I'm gonna find that sonofabitch and make him pay!"

"We was gonna do that bank over in Monett, warn't we?" Daly asked, uneasiness in his voice. "We're getting mighty low on money and—"

"Get 'em ready," Moss interrupted angrily. "We'll hit someplace along the way in Kansas."

"What about me, Mr. Moss?" Wilkins asked, rising from his chair. "It'd be my pleasure to ride with you."

Moss stopped pacing and regarded Wilkins silently for a long period of time, then drew his revolver and fired three shots into the man's chest, each bullet slamming him backward yet he still remained on his feet. Wilkins lived a few moments of shocked surprise before he fell dead to the floor.

Bob Daly stood quietly while the men outside came crowding to the front door. They peered in, not sure whether to enter.

"Why'd you shoot him, Jack?" Daly finally said. "He seemed okay."

"Maybe he was Pinkerton," Moss replied, reloading his revolver. "I didn't like him."

"It wasn't his fault what was in that letter," Daly said. "I think he was okay, who he said he was. We could've used him."

"Shut up about it! It's done and that's all there is to it." Moss holstered his revolver and walked to the door. "Get rid of him." He pushed through the door, the men fearfully stepping aside as he passed on his way outside.

After Moss was gone, three of the men entered and joined Daly, staring at the body.

"Maybe he was Pinkerton," Daly said. "You fellas help me pick him up and take him out of here."

Chapter Eight

On the morning of the third day of practice, Matt was working on his second post, the first having splintered and shattered by repeated hits from his Peacemaker Colts. Now, the interval between shots was shorter and Matt's hand actions smoother as his right thumb pulled the hammer back with less disturbance of the line, his aiming much faster. Not every shot hit the mark, but the misses were close. Matt was delighted with his progress, sure that it indicated a skill he'd actually mastered. Out of the corner of his eye, from behind him, he saw Tom come into the paddock. He half-turned toward him.

"Keep practicing," Tom instructed, his tone severe. "Don't pay any attention to me no matter what I do. You jes' keep on shooting at that post."

Uneasy at the command, wondering why Tom was strolling the circumference of the paddock, Matt concentrated on the post, missing the first shot, but hitting it on the second, third, and fourth.

There was a blur of motion at the periphery of his vision and, instantly, a bullet buzzed past his head, so close that he fell away and dived to the ground. Another bullet skipped the dust no more than three inches from his face. Frantically, he rolled away, seeking cover, finding only a couple of fallen rails.

"Get up!" Tom shouted. "Keep firing at that post!"

"What the hell's going on?" Matt shouted back in anger. "What the hell are you doing?"

"Get up and keep your mind on hitting that post!" Tom repeated. "Go on now!"

Fearfully, Matt rose, looking across the paddock where Tom was holding a revolver, and aimed at him. "Lord, Tom! What are you trying to do?"

"What you've been doing is target practice!" Tom explained. "And that ain't going to be like it really is! You're going have to get used to taking aim when somebody's shooting at you!"

"I'll be damned if I will!"

"I'm pretty good, boy!" Tom assured him. "I ain't likely to hit you, but you're gonna have to learn how to shoot under fire!" Instantly, another bullet whizzed by, ticking at his bowler hat brim.

Without thinking, Matt returned the fire, snapping off a shot at Tom who, somehow miraculously, had stepped away.

"Oh, my God!" Matt cried out. "Tom! I didn't mean to do that!"

"That's all right!" Tom said. "Kinda 'spected it!" He

gestured with his revolver toward the target post. "Now, do what I said! Keep on shooting at that post!"

With a tremulous sigh, Matt turned a shaky aim toward the post. Expecting another shot from his tormentor, he concentrated on the post and squeezed off a shot and missed. Again, he cocked carefully and aimed—a bullet slapped the ground at his feet, another sped past his face—and fired at the post, hitting it.

"Good!" Tom approved. "Keep it up!"

For another ten minutes, they kept at it, the young man making himself take time and deliberate aim at the post, missing more than hitting the mark, and trying not to flinch as Tom's bullets came uncomfortably close.

"That's enough," Tom announced, walking over to join Matt, reloading his revolver. "We'll do this for a few days. You'll get used to it."

"What good does it do?" Matt grumbled, still angry. "I know you're not going to hit me."

Tom raised an eyebrow in a droll expression. "It'll help some. You'll get used to the sound and the feel of it." He paused. "If you're lucky, you might make it."

"You don't think I've got a chance against Moss, do you?"

Tom shrugged. "I don't rightly know what to think. You might not even get a chance for a standup fight. I told you before that Jack is likely to backshoot you from an alley or take you out with a rifle when you're sitting in your living room."

"Then why bother?" Matt said dejectedly.

"Because," Tom said, "you jes' might have some sort of a chance if he does call you out." He nodded at his own wisdom. "That's what we're going to try to do. We're gonna try to figger some sort of a way to play up to his pride." His brows knitted in thought. "Maybe we'll even call him out."

"You're not serious?"

"Depends on how well you do."

"How good is he? Do you know?"

Tom pursed his lips in thought. "I hired on, once, with Jack in some range trouble down in Texas." He shook his head. "He's pretty good, damned fast." He considered his memory for a length of time. "He liked to use that speed to work in close."

"What's that mean?" Matt asked.

"Jes' a guess," Tom told him. "Maybe he ain't too accurate at long-range."

"You don't know that?"

"Nope, I sure don't," Tom admitted.

Matt took a deep breath. "When you say he's fast?"

"Fast draw," Tom explained.

"I draw against him? Is that what I'm supposed to do?"

Tom frowned in response. "What you got to understand is that there jes' ain't no hard and fast rules about all this. Guess it comes from them old ideas about duels. I know it's hogwash, but if it's a callout, there's some that 'spect you to draw against each other. It don't make much sense 'cause after that first shot, it's pretty much whatever you can do to win." He swept his hand away from his body in a dismissive gesture. "I don't know that I'd worry myself too much about what folks 'spect."

"People expect a fair fight, is that it?" Matt asked.

"I don't rightly see that it's fair, what with him being a gunhand and you not."

"When do you teach me to draw?" Matt asked with resolution.

"Guess we might as well start right now."

Matt placed the Colt back in the right holster and poised his hand above it.

"Now!" Tom commanded.

Matt snatched down at the revolver as fast as he could, his hand closing only about the walnut grip, his forefinger missing the trigger guard enclosure as he pulled it from the holster, fumbling it as the revolver came free and fell to the ground.

"Oh, Lordy!" Tom exclaimed.

Chagrined, Matt picked up the Colt, brushed it off and replaced it in his holster.

"Don't wear it quite so low," Tom advised him, showing where his own holsters rode just below the waist on his hips. "Practice slow fer a while," he told him. He half-turned away from Matt, his right arm slightly bent and extended with his hand open and relaxed a couple of inches ahead of the revolver. With a deliberate move, faster than Matt could imagine, Tom's hand came back smoothly and whipped the revolver up, his arm rigidly extended in firing position, unwavering.

"Now, look again," Tom instructed.

This time, he froze his move as his hand came back smoothly to grasp the revolver's grips. "Lay your hand jes' like so, thumbing back that hammer as you clear leather. When she comes up, she'll be ready to go."

He whipped through the rest of the motion and fired the weapon at the post, the bullet smacking into the center of it a foot from the top.

"Now, jes' try putting your hand on 'er," he said. "Nothing more, jes' getting so that them fingers can get comfortable in the right places."

He watched as Matt methodically practiced reaching for and gripping the Colt. Over and over, he touched the weapon, reinforcing the feel of the position. For two hours, he practiced each separate move: touching the weapon, drawing and thumbing the hammer back, raising his arm to aim, firing at the post.

"What do you think?" Matt asked hopefully.

Tom shook his head doubtfully and made a face. "Seems to me that cocking 'er is your trouble. It ain't smooth and it don't look like it's ever gonna be."

"I could have it cocked before I draw," Matt suggested.

Tom gave him a contemptuous look. "And shoot your leg off when you brush that trigger?" He shook his head. "No, we keep on working at it." He squinted up at the noon-high sun. "Long as we got the time."

Chapter Nine

South of Wichita, an elongated trail herd of nearly two thousand Texas cattle raised a huge cloud of dust from the summer-parched plains of Kansas. With little breeze to move it, the haze of fine dirt particles hung over the land. The Wichita & Southwestern Railroad had reached the cattle town in the year of 1873 and lessened the need for longer drives to Baxter Springs in Kansas or to Sedalia, Missouri. Even in the year before the arrival of the railroad over 400,000 cattle had been driven through Wichita to be marketed to buyers. Herd after herd had come up from the cattle ranches of the Southwest, some covering distances of thousands of miles.

Moss and his men had covered their mouths and noses with wet bandannas to keep from choking on the floating grit that enveloped them. At first, the band of outlaws had tried to get ahead of the herd but had only succeeded in converging with the massive obstacle instead of passing it.

"How do drovers stand it?" shouted the muffled voice of the young outlaw, Jimmy, to be heard above the clamorous din of cattle lowings and rumbling hooves.

Moss was on horseback a few feet ahead of the rest of the men watching the cattle, undulating waves of hides and horns moving over the small swells and slopes of the prairie. At times, through the thick haze, cowboys could be seen trying hard to control the strays and contain the periphery of the herd. Bob Daly walked his horse forward to join Moss. "This ain't any good, boss," he said, leaning toward the gang leader. "Let's ride back and get outta this dust and wait till she clears."

"We can cut through," Moss said.

"Maybe," his lieutenant said. "Drovers might think we're rustling. Then, they jes' might take it poorly us making their job tougher for 'em. Either way, there jes' might be some gunplay that we surely don't need."

Moss continued to stare for a time, then shrugged and wheeled his horse, lifting his right hand to signal a retreat. The other members of the outlaw band dug spurs into the sides of their horses to follow Moss and Daly, trotting south away from the herd.

After a couple of miles, the air became easier to breathe and Moss led the group into a small grove of poplars growing on the sides of a lowland stream. They dismounted, slipped the bandannas down around their necks, and led the horses to the stream.

"What do you think?" Moss asked, his manner and voice showing exasperation. "A couple of hours?"

Daly glanced at the sun's late afternoon position in the hazy sky. "They're still strung out quite a ways," he replied. "We could camp here, get a good start in the morning."

"If we don't run into another herd when we get up," Moss said sulkily. "We could drop back and get around 'em. We still got a lot of daylight left."

"The boys are tired and we ought to give the horses a rest. We been pushing pretty hard."

Moss showed a flash of resentment at his henchman's statement and was about to argue then, grudgingly, gave in. "All right," he snapped. Tell 'em we'll spend the night. How we fixed on food?"

"Getting pretty low," Daly told him. "Just what each man's carrying."

"We'll get grub the next town."

"We going into Wichita?"

Moss shook his head. "Like to, but this is a green bunch I got. Wichita's got a couple banks and I don't know that they'd be hard to rob if I had good men, but that ain't the case." He shook his head again. "There's a little place up a ways called Norton. We get provisions there, then move on to Nebraska City."

He placed the stirrup head on the saddle horn, unbuckled the girth strap and removed the saddle from his horse. "Besides, there's bound to be more than a few lawmen in Wichita and Norton ain't likely to have more'n one, if any."

"Ain't likely to have much fer taking, either."

Moss gave his henchman a hard look. "What's that mean?"

Daly's manner became hesitant. "Didn't mean much, boss. It's just that some of the boys are kinda bothered."

"Bothered? What about?" Moss demanded.

"Well, they was kinda counting on doing that bank back there in Missouri, you know."

"That's up to me to decide when and where," Moss said. "Any more does any complaining, they'll be answering to me."

"They ain't exactly complaining, boss," Daly tried to explain. "They . . . all of us . . . we need to get some money, you know."

Moss laid his saddle under a tree and took off the blanket and saddlebags. He led his horse to the stream and tethered it before returning to Daly. "You tell 'em, Bob, that we'll do plenty after I get even for what they've done to my kid brother. They stick by me and they ain't going to have nothing but high times and all the money, they ever thought of. You tell 'em that, Bob."

Daly took a step back away from his leader's intensity. "I'll do that, boss. Right away . . . right away."

Three days later, in the middle of the morning, the Moss gang rode into the ugly little settlement of Norton, Kansas. A few squat, weathered shop buildings, cabins, and sheds on either side of a sunbaked dirt road made up the size of it. Ahead of them, three canvas covered wagons were moving past the western edge of the rural community, new settlers on their way to new land and futures. Two pigs waddled across the road and a cluster of chickens clucked in alarm as the trampling threat of the gang's horses scattered them.

The tallest structure was a livery stable, a barn with a hayloft and a barely readable sign that advertised feed, stabling, and horseshoeing services. Beside it, several horses were standing or slowly ambling in a corral.

"We'll get the horses fed and looked after," Moss said to Daly. He twisted in his saddle and called to his followers. "Take 'em in here, boys!"

The eight men rode to the barn and tied their horses to the hitching rails outside. As they dismounted, a black man came from the open door of the barn.

"We'll be here fer a spell," Moss said, handing the reins of his horse to the stable hand. "This your place?"

"No, suh," the black man replied, his soft, southern speech evident. "Mistuh Fowler. You got to see him befo' I can do anything fo' ya."

"And where do I find Mistuh Fowler?" Moss mocked.

"He 'cross the road there," the stable hand answered, pointing to a gray shanty with a stovepipe emitting smoke over its roof, "having his breakfast."

Moss looked at the building and nodded. "Well, breakfast sounds pretty good, don't it, boys?" He turned back to the black man. "You get started on feeding these animals, boy. We'll go over and have breakfast with your Mistuh Fowler."

The stable hand's eyes swept across the rough crew and sensed malevolence. He nodded. "I get 'em going, suh."

"Take off your saddles and saddlebags," Moss instructed his men. "And don't leave nothing he might steal. Rifles, anything you don't want to lose."

"Hell," said one of the gang, "ain't got anything worth stealing, boss."

Nevertheless, after removing saddles and saddlebags from their horses and stashing them inside the barn, the men carried extra weapons and their few valuables as they strolled across the road to the eatery.

The interior of the shanty enclosed a dining area lined by three long slab tables with benches on either side. Three older men sat at the first table, two on one side, the other across and facing the pair. The men looked up as Moss led a file of men into the building, their conversation interrupted by the boisterous intrusion. At the back of the room, a slab work counter resting on two barrels separated the kitchen from the dining area. A middle-aged woman was at the stove frying meat, an occasional flare of fire producing a sizzle of sound in the frying pans. At another table, a heavyset man and a plain young girl were scrubbing dishes, moving plates, cups, and tableware from a large pan of soapy water into a sudsy rinse in another.

Moss stepped aside as his men rushed past, whooping and being raucous, and took over the two remaining tables. He watched as the girl turned away from the dishwashing, dried her hands, and moved past the counter to greet the new arrivals.

Moss turned to address the three men at the table, all still looking up, curious. "I'm looking for Mr. Fowler," he said in a friendly manner. "One of you gentlemen?"

"I'm Fowler," said the nearest of the two men. He was a large man, likely angular in days gone by, now larded with old age fat around his middle. His face was splotchy with lesions caused by too much sun, deeply lined without an expression of a smile nor a hint of good nature. His hair was white and thinning at the top.

"I'm Jack Yates, Mr. Fowler," Moss said, inventing a last name. With a sidewise nod, he indicated the men at the back tables. "These are my boys. We jes' drove a herd up to these parts."

"Okay," Fowler acknowledged.

"Left our horses over at your stable for feed and to check 'em over," Moss continued, flashing a smile. "Your colored boy over there said to make sure it was all right with you."

"That's William," Fowler said, still not smiling. "He ain't supposed to do nothing till we get money up front."

Moss reached in his pocket and took out a roll of bills. He separated several and laid them beside the empty tin plate in front of Fowler. "This be okay till we have a chance to settle up?"

Fowler looked at the money and a smile of satisfaction creased his weathered face. "Looks to be fine, Mr. Yates. More than enough. I'll go over and—"

"I took the liberty of telling him to go ahead," Moss cut in. "Told him you'd probably tell him to stop if you had other thoughts about it. Was that okay?"

The frown came back to the stable owner. "I guess it's all right. Long as I got the money."

"I'm going to have myself some breakfast," Moss said, walking away. "Thank you and see you later."

Moss joined Daly and two others at the back table just as the young girl came to take their order.

"You all want breakfast or lunch?" she said in a little, whiny voice. She pointed to a large hand-lettered sign posted on the wall above the middle table.

BREAKFAST
Oatmeal
Bacon or Ham
Biscuits & Gravy
Stewed Fruit
Coffee or Milk

LUNCH
Beefsteak and Gravy
Potatoes
Vegetables
Biscuits & Butter
Pie
Coffee or Milk

SUPPER
Beefsteak & Gravy
Potatoes
Vegetables
Cornbread & Butter
Pie
Coffee or Milk

"Take the breakfast, darling," Moss said. "Coffee and you might bring me a piece of whatever pie since it's almost noon."

They lingered over an hour at breakfast, drinking gallons of coffee, some of the younger men trying to flirt with the young girl. She was either a little dimwitted or wisely savvy to cowboy ways and gave no response to their sly comments.

When a couple of the men stood up to leave, the heavyset man came to Moss' table with the bill. "Who gets it?"

"I guess that would be me," Moss said, taking the bill and looking at it. "Seventy-five cents apiece? You're asking a heap . . . them's fancy restaurant prices." He looked up. "You run this place?"

The man nodded. "We charge the going rate. Something wrong with the food?"

"Naw," Moss replied with a nod and a wink. "Damned good chow. You folks do up a meal real fine." He took the money roll from his pocket and counted out the right amount and added another bill. "Something extra for the little girl."

"Thank you," the proprietor said. "That's right kind of you. She'll appreciate it."

"This town . . . you got a lawman?"

"One of those fellas that left awhile ago. The ones you was talking to when you came in."

"Not Mr. Fowler?"

"No, one of the others. Henry Babcock, the one that was sitting across from Fowler. He's the town constable." The man squinted, eyebrows knitting. "Why do you ask?"

"Just curious," Moss told him. "Thought I saw a badge under his vest."

"That's right, he's the constable."

"Well, thank you. See you if we come through again."

Moss and his men left the eatery and walked back to

the livery stable where Fowler and the stable hand were examining one of the horses.

"You got a horse here favoring his right front leg," Fowler said as they entered the barn.

"Your horse, Lige?" Moss asked.

"Yeah," an older man in the group said, stepping forward. "A few miles back, I knowed he kept bowing his head when he stepped on it."

"William noticed it when he brought him in. There waren't nothing like a rock or a sore under his hoof, it might just be a strain," Fowler said. "You might want to lay over a day or so and give it a rest."

"Can't do that," Moss responded. "We gotta keep going."

"Well, maybe we can make a deal here," the stable owner suggested. "It's not a great animal, but I might take him in trade and, for a little extra, sell you one of them out in the corral."

"Sounds like you're getting the better of the deal," Moss countered.

"I'm a fair man."

"It's your horse, Lige," Moss asked. "What do you want to do?"

"Lame horse ain't going do me no good," Lige answered. "Make the trade."

"Our other horses, they okay? All fed and ready for the trail?" Moss asked.

Fowler looked at William and the stable hand gave a quick nod.

"Let's make that an even horse trade, Mr. Fowler," Moss said. "Now, the money I gave you. I'd like it back."

Fowler looked at him, puzzled at the request. "We ain't yet figured out what's due."

"The money," Moss said again, drawing his revolver. "All of it."

The stable owner scowled at the sight of the revolver and he nodded. "I didn't like the looks of you when you came in."

"The money," Moss repeated. "Hand it over."

Fowler took a wallet from his back pocket and started to remove the exact number of bills.

"We'll have it all," Moss said, touching the wallet with the barrel of his revolver. "Everything you've got."

Dutifully, Fowler took the remaining bills from the wallet and handed them to the outlaw. "That's all I got."

"Where do you live?"

Fowler didn't answer.

"Come on, tell me where."

"Out back," Fowler grumbled.

"Lige," the outlaw leader said. "Go out to the corral and pick yourself a new mount. Get a good one." Moss turned to the other members of his gang. "Bob, you and Roscoe go over to the café and get back what I gave 'em. Take everything else they got." He gave a chuckle, then added, "The rest of you go up and down the street and see if the good folks of Norton would like to give us some contributions . . . and if you see them two gentlemen that was having breakfast here with Mistuh Fowler . . . one of 'em is the town lawman."

"Which one, Jack?" one of the gang asked.

"Shoot 'em both if need be, just to be on the safe side," Moss replied. "When you get back, we'll saddle up and head out."

"What are you going to do with me?" Fowler asked.

"We'll mosey back to your house and see what you got stashed away," Moss told him, waving him out the barn door. He turned to the stable hand. "William, what are you going to do while we're gone?"

"Saddle all yo' horses?"

"You got yourself a good boy here, Mistuh Fowler," Jack said.

Thirty minutes later, the Moss gang was on the way to Nebraska City.

"Good horse," Lige told Bob Daly.

"Came out all right," Daly agreed.

Chapter Ten

"Any chance that Matt will be coming home soon, Mr. McKay?" she said in a voice just above a whisper. The young woman lingered while her friends walked out the door, "Hard to say, Miss Carpenter," Ezra replied his own voice low as well. "I know he'll be wanting to get home just as soon as he can."

"Well, if you have a chance to put it in a letter, just tell him that I said hello," she said, a flush of color coming to her face.

"I'll do that, young Miss." He strolled with her to the front of the store and opened the door. "Give your folks my regards," he told her.

The young woman, Elizabeth Carpenter, gave him a gracious smile and walked out to join her friends on the sidewalk. He watched while the three young women walked away.

Nice young lady. Some day, if and when this dreadful thing is well behind us, she just might be the very one for Matt. She'd make a fine daughter-in-law. Pretty as a picture and quite sociable as well. Comes from good, solid Methodist people of considerable substance. She surely would look fine walking down the street with her arm on Matt's. Handsome couple they would be.

He looked out into the twilight street, his eyes searching, seeing nothing but the quiet serenity of the summer evening. Ordinarily, on weekdays he closed the store at six o'clock, but business had been exceptionally brisk today. Steamboat passengers arriving at the Missouri River, some landing, some moving overland from the East, had crowded into this port settlement, buying extra supplies for the journey further west. Nebraska City had become one of the busiest starting points for pioneers seeking new homes, new fortunes, and new opportunities.

Regular customers had also come in, taking time to browse, wanting to talk, wanting to know where Matt had gone and, like the young Miss Carpenter, wondering when he'd be coming home again.

A few still wanted to talk about the shooting and a couple of spiteful blowhards had made sarcastic comments that the killing had scared Matt out of town.

"Is he hiding out somewhere till they catch Moss, Ezra?" the final customer, a town lawyer, asked with a hint of derision. "Probably smart of him."

"Be smart of you not to ask," McKay responded, not caring at all if he gave offense.

"Didn't mean anything, Ezra."

"Sure you didn't," McKay said, walking the lawyer to the door, making it clear that he should leave.

"Meant nothing at all," the lawyer muttered and walked swiftly out.

McKay took another look at the nearly deserted street. *Nothing suspicious.*

He grunted, swung the door shut, turned the key in the lock and shoved the deadbolt into place. He pulled the window shades down and walked through the gloomy shop toward the lantern on the back counter and took one more look around. Satisfied, he lit the lamp and started up the stairway to the living quarters above the store.

It was a lonely life. Wife gone for several years and, now, the boy.

Probably the best idea that Matt's gone. Patterson's right about that. Probably right about hiring somebody to kill Moss too.

At the top of the steps, he opened the door into the residence rooms, the light of his lantern invading the darkness.

Behind him, the door slammed shut!

McKay turned in panic to see a heavily built, ugly man standing behind him, a revolver aimed at his chest.

"Good evening, Mr. McKay," came a voice from another direction.

Bewildered and frightened, McKay swung around to see a tall, bearded man step from the dark into the light, his shadow looming large on the wall behind him. Compared to his companion, he was nicely dressed, a dark-hued alpaca coat over his shoulders, a near-new Stetson pushed back on his head to reveal a lock of brown hair.

"Let me help ya with that lamp," the man behind him

said almost pleasantly. He reached to take the lantern from McKay's hand and placed it on a nearby table.

"Jack Moss?" McKay asked, his voice betraying his fear.

"And my friend, Bob Daly," the dapper outlaw said, pointing to the man holding the revolver. He gestured to the rear of the residence. "We came up the fire escape. Mighty careless of you to leave a window open." He nodded to a chair. "Sit down and let's have a talk."

"What do you want?" McKay asked tremulously.

"Well, our quarrel ain't directly with you," Moss said. "I'd like to see your son."

"He's not here."

"We know that," Moss said softly. "We've been looking around for him." He gestured again to the chair and, with moderate force, eased the older man into it. "Where'd he go?"

"I won't tell you that."

Moss pulled up a straight-backed chair and positioned it in front of McKay. He sat down, leaning forward, his face sinister in the flickering lamplight. "That whelp of yours killed my kid brother," he said in a low, intimidating voice. "I don't know that I should let you live . . . you sired the bastard . . . but the only chance you have is to tell me where he's gone."

McKay set his mouth in a firm line, glaring at the outlaw. "It was your brother's fault! He shot first! Matt was just defending himself."

"My brother was drunk!" Moss said sharply. "Just having himself a good time. You see what that shotgun did to him? I want your son!"

"Go to hell!"

"In time, I suppose," Moss said, leaning back. He studied the man in front of him. "One more chance."

"You'll kill me anyway," McKay countered. "You'll not get it from me." He jerked his head at the man with the gun. "Go ahead, get it over with."

Moss reacted slowly, almost languidly. He reached into his coat pocket to take out a hunting knife in a scabbard. He unbuttoned the strap around the handle and took out the knife. He turned it in the light, letting the reflection of the burnished blade dance in the dark corners of the room. He touched the sharp edge and made a face as though wounded by the slightest touch.

"You'll tell, old man," the outlaw assured him. "Maybe in five minutes, maybe in an hour, but you'll tell."

Ezra McKay lunged toward Moss, then felt the blow that crashed down on his head from behind. Stunned, he felt something wrap around his arms, pinning him to the chair. Then came the rough hands stuffing something into his mouth, a gag nearly suffocating him.

Then, as his senses began to return, he felt the first searing slice of the knife on his face.

Chapter Eleven

The two men came into the Gold Strike just as J. C. Farley started lighting the wall lamps to brighten the saloon's interior as daylight faded into dusk. They came in quietly and unobtrusively, moving first to the bar where they waited patiently for J. C. to return, then ordered drinks. The slim young man was not more than twenty-five with a pale, thin beard and dirty-blond hair spilling out from under a stained, short-crowned hat. His trail-soiled companion was a portly middle-ager who walked with a rolling limp.

"Where you from, gentlemen?" J. C. asked as he poured their whiskies.

"Take a little water with that." The younger one spoke in a take-charge manner. "Come up from Texas and thereabouts."

"Business here?" the bartender asked.

"Nope," the young man replied. "Just riding around, no place special." He looked around the saloon, which was becoming active, the evening customers arriving. He looked up the flight of steps to the upper floor. "You got rooms here?"

"You mean like a hotel?" J. C. countered carefully, then shook his head. "There's a rooming house down the street and there's tents just a little past where you can get a cot for the night."

"Saw the rooming house when we come in," the older man spoke up. "Didn't suit our fancy." He glanced at his companion and smirked. "And we ain't sleeping in no cootie tent either."

J. C. gave a nod. "Well, we could surely use a good hotel here and I reckon it'll happen one of these days." He sighed in commiseration. "Gold Stream's not much more than a mining camp right now and you'll have to make do with what we got, I suppose." He smiled at them. "I'd try the rooming house. It may not look like much, but beds are clean and they're better than sleeping on the ground."

The young man returned his gaze to the stairway as Betty and two other young women came down the steps, ready to begin their evening's work. "Looks like you got rooms up there."

"Just the owner's apartment and a few rooms for employees," J. C. said evasively.

"Sporting house, is it?" the young man said with a trace of mockery that hadn't been there before. He nodded to Betty as she came to the bottom of the steps and started mingling with the men at the tables. "She one of your . . . what did you call 'em? Employees?"

The bartender seemed not to hear the question. "Let me freshen your drinks there," he said congenially, pouring from the bottle into each of their glasses. "On the house."

"If I'd make it right," the young man said, sipping the whiskey from the brim, "suppose I could get a good night's sleep after I'd take that one back up to bed?"

The bartender's smile had disappeared and he found work to do behind the bar, glasses to be washed. "Let me know if you want something more or when you're ready to settle up, gentlemen." He moved away down the bar to strike up conversation with two of his regulars.

The newcomers seemed not to take offense at the bartender's change in manner. They carried their glasses to a nearby table and sat down, talking in low voices. After awhile, they signaled to J.C. who brought a bottle to their table and filled their glasses once again. Then, they went back to their quiet conversation.

Joe Calvecci came down the stairway, his eyes sweeping the room, noting the composition of the clientele. He spotted the newcomers at once. "Who are they?" he asked J.C. as he came to the bar, nodding to the two at the table.

"Didn't introduce themselves," J.C. responded with a trace of hesitation. "Riding through from down around Texas. Don't know where they're heading." He gave a small shake of his head.

"Trouble?"

"None that I can see," the bartender said. "Asked about where to spend the night. Didn't want to try the rooming house or the tents."

"Can't say that I blame them."

"Had their eyes on our upstairs," J.C. told him. "The

younger feller wanted to pay for Miss Betty." He paused. "I didn't much like the way he said it."

Calvecci looked at the two men, trying to size them up. Finally, he turned back to his bartender. "Looks like they're minding their own business. Being strangers in town, they'd just not know how we run our place. I expect they'll be moving out before long."

"Hope so," the bartender ventured, his eyes shifting from his employer to the two men. "There's something about the younger one."

"It'll be all right," Calvecci assured him. "I don't think there'll be any trouble." He smiled and walked away. "I've always had a good nose for trouble, you know."

"Hope you're right, boss," J. C. whispered to himself. "Somehow, I think you ain't."

Betty and the younger women were circulating. Wanda and Pauline were more spirited in their flirtations, a little bawdier in their actions and banter. Betty moved in a more sedate manner, speaking low and affably to her many friends. She never stayed with one for very long, declining the many invitations to sit with this man or the next, refusing gracefully the offer of drinks, moving from table to table.

"Miss!"

Betty was turning to the voice when a hand grasped her wrist with punishing strength. She tried to pull away, angered at the young man who held her, offended by his insolent smile. "Let me go," she said in a tight, controlled voice. "Let me go this instant."

"Just want you to sit down and give us a little of your

company," the young man said with a pretended civility. "My name's Bill Deiter, what's yours?"

Betty eased down into a chair, expecting the man to release her, surprised that he did not.

"I think you'd jump up and run away if I let you loose," he said. "Done that kinda trick before, ain't you?"

Betty glanced from the young man to the other, hoping he'd intervene.

The older man gave a shrug of indifference. "He does just about whatever he wants. You know what's good fer ya, better go along."

"You're hurting my wrist," Betty said, returning her cool gaze to the man, Deiter.

The young man gave a look of mock concern and shifted his hand to hold hers. "Mighty sorry, ma'am. That better?"

"You can let go," Betty responded. "I won't run."

Deiter gave her questioning smile, then released her hand. "I didn't get your name."

"I don't think you'll have a need for it," she countered, her gaze shifting over Deiter's shoulder, hoping to catch J. C.'s eyes.

He was at the far end of the bar and busy with a customer.

Betty leaned back in her chair, affecting an ease of manner. She'd dealt with roughnecks and the overly amorous before and a seeming compliance usually worked better than to provoke anger. "You here for gold?"

Deiter gave her a bright smile and shook his head. "Too damned much work for what little you get out of a pan or digging out a hole." He looked at his companion. "Say, this here's Merle. You got another whore around here for him too?"

Betty's eyes narrowed, but she showed no other sign of resentment. Abruptly, she lunged out of her chair, crying out in pain as Deiter caught her by the arm and threw her back.

"Oh, excuse me," Deiter feigned apology. "I 'spect you took that badly. Waren't at all nice of me, was it?"

Over his shoulder, she could see that Calvecci was now watching. After a moment, he stepped down from his high perch chair and walked quickly into a back room. A few moments later, he reappeared with a couple of young husky miners who earned evening money by handling troublemakers. She relaxed, relieved as she saw the two brawlers moving ahead of Calvecci as they strode toward her.

Deiter followed her look and turned, lazily, to see the men approach. "No closer, boys," he said, remaining in his chair, contempt sharing his tone of command.

The trio stopped.

"Just talking business with this lady," Deiter said amiably. "About how much she charges." He peered between the two big men at the proprietor. "What's your cut, old man?"

One of the bouncers took a step forward with a no-nonsense attitude. "I think it's time—"

A gun appeared in Deiter's hand as if willed there and exploded a shot.

With a cry of pain, the bouncer fell to the floor, thrashing in pain as he grasped at his right leg. Then, fear replaced his anguish and he began to drag himself across the floor, away from the man with the gun.

The other bouncer and Calevecci stood very still.

"Now, look what you've done," Deiter said to Betty. "I come in fer a nice evening, looking to have a little fun from you ladies and you go and spoil it all."

"He wasn't carrying a gun," Betty exclaimed.

"But he was bigger'n me, now wasn't he?" Deiter said and laughed. He turned to the older man who'd leaped to his feet at the gunshot. "Sit down, Merle. There ain't gonna be no more trouble." He returned his gun to his holster and raised his hands in a counterfeit gesture of appeal. "Everybody just mind your own business."

Apprehensively, the other brawler reached down to help his comrade, half-lifting, half-dragging the injured man away. Two other men, equally fearful, helped to bear the gunshot victim out of the saloon.

Calvecci took a step forward. "You intend to shoot me too?"

Deiter chuckled. "Naw, you're too old and too puny."

"Then you'd better leave."

"Why?" Deiter rose to his feet. "You gonna call a lawman?"

Calvecci hesitated. "Not exactly."

Deiter exchanged an amused glance with his burly companion. "What's that supposed to mean? You got a lawman or don' cha?"

Calvecci didn't answer.

Betty gave a slight, nearly imperceptible shake of her head, but Deiter caught it.

"You *do* have somebody!" Deiter exclaimed in

delight. He turned to regard Betty. "Somebody thinks you're pretty special, maybe?" He stepped closer to her. "You got some feller taking care of you?"

Her defiant eyes met his.

Again, the revolver flashed into Deiter's hand as a gasp came from the onlookers. For a moment, he held it at an angle, the muzzle pointed at the ceiling. Then, he brought the gun barrel across in a vicious sweep, slamming it into the side of Betty's face as she tried to turn away, a bloody gash instantly appearing on her upper cheek and temple. She fell, unconscious, sprawling out, sending a chair flying as she collapsed on the floor.

For a few seconds, no one moved.

From across the room, Wanda and Pauline rushed to Betty, ignoring the gunman. Wanda cradled the unconscious woman in her arms, brushing back her hair to examine the wound. She looked up at Deiter, anger in her face and voice. "You'll be a sorry sonofabitch when he hears about this."

"That's interesting, girl," Deiter said, returning his revolver to his holster. "Whoever he is, you all must think he's something pretty nasty." He gestured to Betty. "I 'spect that ought to bring him running." He looked around, scanning faces. "If her fancy man decides to do something, tell him to bring a gun."

"What do you want?" Calvecci demanded. "No one in this town's done anything to you."

Again, the young man lifted his hands in a gesture of feigned innocence. "We're just a couple of drifters, looking to have a good time, that's all. She could've been nicer to me and nothing would have happened."

He reached down and pulled Pauline away from Betty, dragging her to her feet. "I'll take this one," he announced to Calvecci. "She ain't as pretty as . . ." He paused and looked down at the unconscious girl on the floor as Wanda accepted a wet cloth from J.C. and wiped away the blood. "Well, maybe she's just as pretty as that. Maybe more, now."

Deiter gave the girl a shove toward the stairway, the crowd parting before them as he pushed her along. "Take the other if you've a mind to, Merle," he called. "See you in the morning." With a rush, he took the steps two at a time, pulling Pauline with him as she struggled against him. In a few moments, they were out of sight, then Pauline's pleas and shouts were diminished by the slamming of an upstairs door.

Deiter's companion took a step toward the saloon owner, giving a nod of his head to Betty who was beginning to stir, a small moan coming from her. "Sorry about the lady," the burly man said. "Like he said . . . maybe if she'd just come along quiet." He wagged his head.

"He'll answer for this," Calvecci muttered.

"I'd not cross him if I was you," Merle said with a somber face, pointing up the stairs. "Now, if that gal don't give him no sass, she'll be none the worse for it by tomorrow." He motioned to the door. "Then, we'll probably be outta here first thing in the morning." He turned away, then turned back to Calvecci with another thought. "You decide you want to get somebody to get even, you'd better think it over hard. I ain't never seen more than a couple of gunhands any faster or meaner than him. Best you just let things be."

"What's he looking for?" Calvecci asked. "To kill somebody?"

The man nodded. "He likes it."

Calvecci looked at him, sizing him up.

"People are afraid of him," Merle continued. "Do anything he asks. Give him anything he wants." He gave a grunt of wry mirth. "He scares me too."

"Then . . . why do you ride with him?"

The man gave a crooked smile. "Whatever he takes, whatever folks give him, there's always plenty for me too." He pointed at Wanda attending to Betty. "Whenever she's done, send her on up to me."

As the burly man limped up the steps, individuals in the crowd began to move toward the entrance doors, many of them hurrying. Only a couple remained to help the owner and the bartender reset the tables and chairs, then they, too, scurried out of the building.

"Take her up to my apartment," Calvecci instructed J. C. and Wanda. "I'll get someone to look after her face." He took a step closer, bent down to the girl and pointed to the stairway. "You don't have to go, you know that."

Wanda looked up at the upper level of the saloon, then shook her head. "Thanks, Joe, but I'll be okay. Might head off any trouble if I just go along."

Calvecci gave the girl's arm an affectionate squeeze, then turned back to J. C. as Wanda helped Betty toward the stairs.

"Think you'd better fetch Tom?" J. C. asked.

"That's what the bastards want," Calvecci replied. "I don't know . . . he's damned fast."

"Too fast for Tom?"

Calvecci didn't answer immediately, deep in thought. "Let's give it some time. Maybe they'll just go on their way. No use in getting somebody killed.

"I got a bad feeling, boss. The young one wants to do some killing and he's gonna do someone."

Calvecci gave a slow nod. "If they don't leave by morning, I'll send Charlie up to get Tom. If he's been at the bottle, it might give him time enough to sober up.

Chapter Twelve

In the late afternoon of the eighth day, they stood facing each other across the corral.

"Draw!" Tom commanded.

His gun was aimed at Matt before the latter could react.

"Too slow, boy! Jack Moss will have three shots in you before you clear leather!"

Dejectedly, Matt returned the Colt to his holster and poised his arm once again, waiting for the signal.

Instead, without a word, Patterson turned and walked toward the ranch house.

"Are we quitting?" Matt called. "Or what?"

"Just stay there," Tom instructed as he entered the house. "Be with you in a minute."

In more like five, he was back, carrying a heavy handgun at his side. "Let's see what you can do with this one," he said, handing the massive revolver to Matt.

"What's this?" Matt asked, accepting the weapon, dismayed at the heft of it.

"Walker Colt," Tom informed him, nodding with satisfaction at the revolver. "Black powder load . . . needs some extra time to fix up your loads." He took another cylinder from his pocket and displayed it. "When you run out, you'll have to replace the whole wheel."

"This is an old gun," Matt protested, raising it to aim.

"She's old," Tom agreed, "but she's in good shape. Designed for and named for Captain Samuel Hamilton Walker of the Texas Rangers."

"I can hardly lift it," Matt complained, half in jest. "Much less aim it." He lowered the revolver in a motion of rejection. "What's the use of it?"

"Well, get used to 'er," Tom instructed. "It might just give you an edge with Moss."

"How? Lord knows, it's going to slow me down."

"You ain't ever going to outdraw Jack Moss," Tom said. "Like I told you, he likes to work in close and this old Walker will stop a man a dozen paces farther away than them Peacemakers."

"Meaning what?"

"You draw on him when he's in your range, not the other way round," Tom said cheerfully.

"Some edge," Matt said ruefully.

"Nothing's for sure," Tom admitted. "If there's a whisker of a chance, then, maybe, this old blaster will do the job." He glanced across the corral at the shot-splintered posts, then looked to another at a greater distance away. "We'll start all over," he said with a solemn deliberation. "Aim at that post over there."

"Draw and fire?" Matt asked with pained reluctance.

"Naw, just see if you can hit the damned thing."

They stood in the corral, Matt trying to adjust to the feel of the heavier weapon. He cocked, sighted and fired, the Walker bucking in his hand, his first six shots missing the target. Changing the cylinder was an awkward and time-consuming task.

"I can imagine what Moss is doing while I'm fumbling around with this," Matt said.

"Hell, if you can't get him with your first six, you're gone anyway," Tom chortled. "Just take your time."

Tom showed him how to reload the cylinders, tamping the black powder down into the weapon. "You'll need to clean 'er often," he instructed. "She'll foul up if you don't."

It was slow work and frustrating. Matt hit the post for the first time on the third shot of his third load. To his astonishment, the top of the post exploded in a spray of splinters.

"She'll do some damage," Tom said in wry comment. "If you can put up with all the fuss and bother." He turned and sauntered toward the ranch house. "Think I'll get myself out of the sun."

About an hour later, Patterson roused from his doze in his chair, aware of something unusual, something different. Then, he heard it again; the heavy report of the Walker blended with the solid thwack of the bullet hitting a target. "Three in a row?" Tom marveled aloud. "Can't be." He rose and hurried to the side door to look out at the corral.

Matt was replacing the big Colt into his holster, his position reversed since Tom had seen him last. Now, the young man was presenting his left profile to the target with the holstered gun on his right hip away from it. As Tom watched, Matt made an almost languid move, drawing the Walker, flinging it across his chest, his left hand coming up to catch his right, steadying his aim as he fired. This time, the bullet missed its mark, but not by much as it ticked at the side of the post.

"What the hell are you doing?" Tom demanded as he charged to the corral. "That ain't no way to shoot!"

Matt turned, startled at Tom's intrusion and chagrined by his anger. "It seems to work," he said. "Why isn't it?"

"I never saw nobody ever shoot a gun like that," Patterson railed. "Two hands?" He shook with indignation. "Why, that'd be something you'd expect a girl to do."

Matt grinned at the reprimand. "Thought you said I should do whatever it takes." He tucked his left arm against his side and slapped his gun hand into his left palm, sighted and fired. This time, the bullet hit the post squarely, the impact breaking the post in half, the top section falling to the ground.

"Takes too long," Tom said sharply. "And it ain't a fair way to fight."

"You said I wouldn't ever outdraw Moss," Matt countered. "I figured a true shot might be better than a fast one."

"If you ain't going to take my advice, then just hand over that piece and be on your way."

"I'll go if you say, Tom," Matt said affably. "I'll keep the Walker if you don't mind. I'd say we'd more than paid for it."

"Well, take it and be damned," Tom said. "You get yourself killed and—"

"Hold up, Tom," Matt said, his eyes upon something in the distance. "Somebody's coming."

Tom turned, following Matt's gaze.

Across the mountain meadow, a man was riding at a gallop.

"Charlie Meacham," Tom identified the rider. "Wonder what he wants?"

The old man rode into the paddock, reining the horse to a stop. "They need you in town, Tom," Charlie Meacham declared in a dry, almost whispering voice.

"Who's they, Charlie?" Tom asked.

"Mr. Calvecci sent me," Charlie said, his voice a little stronger to emphasize the importance of the summons. "We got a couple of bad 'uns in town, one special bad. Mr. Calvecci said to come."

Tom didn't immediately respond. "You got Dutch Snyder," he said gruffly.

The old man shook his head. "Not so that you'd know it. Ain't seen a sign of Dutch since they rode in."

Tom shrugged. "Best jes' let them be, then. Don't cross 'em and, chances are, they'll jes' ride on outta town and be somebody else's problem."

Again, the old man shook his head. "Don't think so, Tom. They don't seem in any hurry, jes' hanging around town looking for trouble. One of 'em, he shot

Gus Aldrich in the leg somethin' terrible and. . . ." He paused.

"And what, Charlie?"

"Pistol whipped one of the girls at the Gold Strike."

A frown of concern came to Tom's face. "Betty?"

The old man pursed his lips and grimaced before answering. "She's all right, but. . . will you come?"

Tom remained silent. After a few moments, he asked, "Will Calvecci pay?"

"For God's sake, Tom!" Matt exploded. "What are you asking?"

Tom ignored him, his eyes on Charlie Meacham.

"I'd guess so, Tom," the old man said, nodding his head, "if the job's done right."

"You ride on back to town and tell that Eye-talian to have it ready," Tom commanded. "Nate's place. I'll be along directly."

The elderly man gave him a curt nod in response, turned his horse and spurred it away. "As soon as you can, Tom," he called back over his shoulder.

"I can't believe you!" Matt said angrily. "Miss Betty's been good to you—"

"I'd have gone without the money," Tom cut in. "But Calvecci don't need to know that and he can afford it." He turned toward the ranch house. "You stay—"

"I'll go with you," Matt broke in.

Tom started to argue, then shrugged. "Do what you please."

"You don't know his name or anything about him," Matt said, the thought coming to him.

"Ain't important. If'n he's better'n me, I'd jes' as soon not know it."

"Why's that?" Matt asked, astonished.

" 'Cause I'd be thinking too much about it," Tom replied cheerfully. "Come on, let's go."

Chapter Thirteen

Five of them met in the small room at the back of the Nate's store; Charlie, Matt, Wainscote standing, Tom and Calvecci seated at a rough table.

Calvecci cleared his throat. "A couple of them rode into town yesterday evening and came up into my place just after suppertime. They seemed all right at first, quiet and minding their own business." He gave an apologetic shrug. "I've been in the business a long time and I should've spotted trouble sooner." He paused to organize his thoughts. "They started drinking heavy after awhile and bothering the young ladies. Wanted to take Betty upstairs and got rough about it when she didn't want to go."

"How bad?"

Calvecci frowned. "The younger one laid open her scalp under her hair on the right side with his pistol and bruised her up on the face." He shook his head. "She didn't lose any teeth but not because he didn't try."

"Name's Deiter," Charlie said, anxious to be a part of the telling. "Bill Deiter."

Calvecci gave the old man an annoyed look, then turned to Tom. "Ever hear of him?"

Tom shook his head. "How about the other one?"

"Older man, pushing fifty, I'd say," Calvecci answered. "Heavyset, walks with a bit of a limp. I heard Deiter call him Merle—"

"Merle Varney," Tom cut in with a tone of derision. "Hung out in Texas for a spell."

"Gunfighter?" Nate Wainscote asked.

"Backshooter," Tom replied scornfully. "Most owl-hoot gangs would tolerate him for a while, then even them would get sick of him and kick him out."

Calvecci took a wallet from his coat and removed several bills. "All I could lay my hands on in a hurry, Tom," he said. "Will that do?"

Tom took the bills. "Burying money, I guess. They still at your place?"

Calvecci nodded.

"Might as well get at it," Tom said and rose from his chair. "Give me a few minutes, then tell 'em I'm calling 'em out. I'll be on the street waiting for them."

Calvecci rose and shook his hand. "Good luck, Tom," he said, then walked out of the room.

Tom turned to Matt and handed him the money. "Give this to Betty if something should happen," he said, then lowered his voice. "Most of your pa's money's is in a can behind the coffee on the shelf."

"I couldn't take it back," Matt sputtered.

Tom was already walking away, drawing one revolver out of his right holster to check it, then the other from his left as he strode through the open front door.

Matt, Nate, and Charlie rushed after him.

"Best stay inside," Tom cautioned them as he settled into one of the three wooden chairs in the shade of the building. "They'll be coming out any time." He rocked the chair back against the wall and balanced there, his heels hooked over the lower brace. He sat quietly for a while, resting his head against the roughly cut siding, his eyes surveying the field of battle.

Earlier in the day, there had been the usual bustle of men on horses, driving and unloading freight wagons or strolling the plank walks. Now, only a few were hurrying by, anxious to get inside buildings to safety. Across the street at the lumberyard, half-loaded wagons had been left unattended. Activity in the adjacent freight office had ceased. In front of it, another wagon had been partially unburdened, crates abandoned in the roadway.

The street was deserted and very quiet.

"They're coming out, Tom," Nate called from the doorway where he and Matt were standing.

"Best get behind something there in the store," Tom advised them. "There may be some stray bullets."

Four buildings away, Deiter and Varney walked warily from the door of the Gold Strike. They separated immediately, Deiter sprinting to the other side of the street, the older man coming cautiously on the plank walk toward the Gold Stream Mercantile. Neither had spotted Tom yet as he sat in the shade of the building. Each man's eyes were searching all building corners, every doorway, each alley. The younger man stepped nimbly, his movements quick and decisive as he advanced. He wore his gun belt with a revolver in a single holster high on his hip, his right hand crooked at his waist, ready to draw. The other man, older, limped slowly down Tom's side of the street, his right hand curled around the revolver he wore at his side.

"Merle Varney!" Tom called. "You know what's best, turn now and walk away!"

Varney stopped walking and stood twenty-five yards away, his head moving quickly from side to side, trying to locate the voice. Then, he stared into the shadow of the mercantile building. Across the street, Deiter had also spotted Tom and paused in a defensive stance.

"Patterson?" Varney's voice held a note of disbelief. "Tom Patterson?"

"You really want a part of this, Varney?" Tom asked, rocking forward and rising to his feet. He stepped off the plank walk, careful to keep the hitching post and rail between himself and the watchful man across the street. "Better wait back in the saloon till your partner does the job, Merle. If he don't get 'er done, you got a chance to get outta town before I head that way."

The heavyset man actually took a step backward in a mincing manner, it was almost comical. "Hell, Bill!" he called to the younger man, his voice a plea. "I ain't going up against Tom Patterson." He directed his appeal to Tom. "Didn't know it was you, Tom. I ain't got no quarrel with you."

"Back out then, if you got such a mind," Tom said, his full attention on the man opposite him who was moving slowly, nonchalantly into the street.

"You don't stand with me, you're for sure a dead man, Merle," Deiter called to the frightened man. "Better play the odds."

Varney looked from one to the other, frozen in desperate indecision.

"So, the famous Tom Patterson," Deiter said pleasantly, edging forward on the street. "I never figured that I'd get a chance to—"

Tom darted to his left anticipating Deiter's swift draw, his own Colt flashing into his right hand as Deiter's fusillade thundered into the storefront wall, just missing him. Tom hit the ground, his own revolver speaking once, twice, three times as he rolled to his feet in a crouch.

Across the street, Deiter, firing wildly, was scurrying for cover behind the wagon and the stacks of unloaded crates beside it.

Tom, hunkering down, ran to his right to the low cover of a water trough and snapped a shot into the back wheel of the wagon.

A bullet from Varney's direction cut into Tom's right side, causing a sudden jolt that turned into a searing pain. Tom uttered a grunt at the pain and ignored the second bullet that fanned past his face. He aimed carefully at Merle Varney's ample midsection and put two shots just above his belly button, but didn't wait to see the desperado fall.

He pulled his other Colt, his eyes searching for Deiter. The gunman was well hidden behind the wagon and the crates. Even so, Tom could see his enemy's shadow move, a disadvantage that Deiter might not have realized.

Two more shots came from Deiter's gun, then a pause in the firing.

Reloading. Time for me to do the same.

Tom laid his second gun close by as he fed bullets into the near-empty cylinder of his first. He glanced to his right and saw that Merle Varney had sunk to his knees, his head down as though staring at the blood that seeped through his fingers from his belly. As Tom watched, the man toppled forward and lay still in the dust.

He snapped the cylinder back into place, took a quick look at the blood soaking his shirt from his own wound, then peeked around the right side of the trough.

The shadow was no longer there.

Despite the swelling pain in his side, Tom moved his body closer to the trough and cursed himself for poor judgment.

Took my eyes off of him and he moved!

Tom considered the vulnerability of his water trough protection and didn't like it. *If he gets on this side of the street, I'm a dead man! Did he go to my right or my left?*

He scanned the empty street to his right and saw no sign of the gunman or any likely place of concealment.

Behind me!

Tom lunged to the end of the trough just as bullets punched into the ground he'd vacated. Risking a look over the trough, he saw Deiter's head peeking momentarily around the corner of the mercantile building. Tom ducked as Deiter began firing again, his shots thumping through the water trough.

Tom crawled forward along the trough and aimed his revolver to just a few inches right of the building edge.

He let loose a steady barrage of shots, spacing each one erratically, hoping to catch Deiter as the gunman leaned out to return fire.

Suddenly, there was a loud cry of pain followed by a stream of anguished oaths. "Hold your fire, Patterson! I'm hit!" Deiter called out. "I'm hit bad!" His revolver arced out from behind the building into the dust of the street. "Don't shoot! I'm coming out."

Deiter reeled from behind the building, bowed over in apparent pain, his left hand clutching his chest, the other hand dangling limply at his side. "I'm hurt bad and I ain't got a gun, Patterson," he called, walking unsteadily forward, contrite, beginning to bring his right hand up in an appeal. "You wouldn't shoot an unarmed man!"

Tom shot him twice, then a third time for good measure. "Don't count on it," he said aloud.

In the store, Matt stared through the window in disbelief, a swell of disgust overwhelming him.

Tom rose from behind the trough and took a few steps forward to look at Deiter's sprawled figure, close enough to see the look of astonishment on the dead man's face. From inside the buildings, the Gold Strike and the tent saloons, and from the spaces between the buildings, the first cluster of townspeople, miners, and cowhands came out of their shelters. At first moving tentatively, then in a rush, everyone was eager to gawk at the fallen bodies. As more came out, they formed a ragged circle around Tom, wanting to rush up in congratulations, though nervous at the sight of the gun still in his hand.

Slowly, he holstered the gun, took a step toward the

mercantile building, then stopped abruptly, sagged a bit, bending over in pain.

Nate and Charlie were the first to reach him, Matt trailed closely behind them.

"You bad hurt, Tom?" Nate asked.

"I can't tell," Tom said, gingerly touching his side, wincing as he examined the wound. "Losing some blood." He pursed his lips and pressed his shirt against the wound. "May have gone plumb through." He looked around. "Charlie, get me up to that Chi-nee barber. He may not let on that he knows about doctoring but I got the notion he'll probably know a sight more than anyone else."

With Charlie under his left shoulder, Tom threw his right arm over a well-wisher's back. "Careful as you go, fella," he admonished the man. "Don't go knocking into me."

With Tom between them, the two men half-walked, half-dragged the wounded gunfighter through the crowded streets, the throng moving with them, the voices of the onlookers cheering the progression.

"Good for you, Tom!"

"You took 'em, boy! Two on one . . . and you took 'em!"

"Not to worry, Tom! Ain't nothing but a scratch!"

"Kilt 'em both, he did!"

Nate Wainscote looked down at Matt. "He'll be all right," he said reassuringly.

"I'm sure of it," Matt responded, a trifle brusque.

Nate caught the intonation. "Something bothering you?"

Matt nodded his acknowledgment.

Nate regarded the young man for a long moment, then motioned for Matt to follow. "Come with me," he ordered.

He led the young man across to the knot of people crowding around Deiter, easing through the circle with Matt following. "Check his hand, boy," the big man instructed, "his right hand."

Despite a moment of repugnance, Matt reached for the gunman's right hand and turned it over. In the movement, the lax dead fingers released the small derringer.

Matt looked at Wainscote, a different expression on his face. "Then . . . Tom knew?"

"Did or didn't . . . it don't bother me one way or another," Nate said pointedly. He started after the procession. "Coming along?"

With only a moment's hesitation, Matt fell into step with the larger man's stride, stretching his legs to keep up as they hurried away.

"We've put him up for the night upstairs," Betty told Matt, gesturing to the upper hall. She smiled, the facial movement bringing pain from the deep bruise on her cheek. "There's a room for you there too."

Matt looked up the stairway with some misgivings. "I don't know that—"

"You don't have to have anybody," Betty cut in, amused. "Wanda's gonna give you her bed."

"Where'll she sleep?" he asked, gesturing to the buxom young woman.

"I done find myself a place," Wanda giggled. "You get lonely, though, you jes' holler and I'll come a-running!"

Betty gave her a friendly slap on the rump to send

her on her way back into the saloon, then took Matt's arm and started him up the steps. "Think that bullet went clean through, didn't hurt a thing as far as that Chinese barber could see." She caught his eye and gave him a wink. "Lucky for us here in Gold Stream, I think that Chinese feller is a whole lot better than the barber he pretends to be." She touched her scalp. "Sewed me up slick as a whistle and only charged two bits."

"Did you watch?"

"The gunfight?" she answered, then shook her head. "I couldn't." She paused, then added: "I mean. . . I could've, but I wouldn't."

Matt nodded his understanding, then asked, "Any idea of how long Tom will be laid up?"

"Well, he said he was going to ride home tomorrow," she confided, her voice betraying her doubt. "I don't know as how he could." She shook her head. "He's going to be weak as a cat, losing all that blood." She gave him a slight push up the stairs. "You go on up, now."

Matt undressed reluctantly, down to his ankle-length drawers, but no further. He washed the dust of the day from his face, neck, and hands at the washbasin, mindful of the many who'd preceded him at it. He scrubbed at his teeth with a finger, doing the best as he could without a brush, unwilling to make use of the one that hung from a string on the washbasin chest.

Finally, he puffed out the kerosene lamp and, with the dim light flickering through the open transom, he lay upon Wanda's bed. It was softer than he could've imagined, a hair mattress from the feel of it, and far more comfortable than the one at Patterson's ranch. The pillows were stuffed with feathers, a faint and not unpleasant perfume wafting from them. Matt laid his head back upon it and stared up at the ceiling, watching the dancing patterns cast through the transom by the guttering hallway lamp. He listened to the distant sounds of music and laughter in the saloon below, and, twice, heard the quick light steps coming up the stairway followed by the hasty clump of boots in rapid pursuit. There were whispers and giggles in the hall, doors opening and closing, springs squeaking, squeals and excited exclamations in adjacent rooms. He closed his eyes, too drowsy to listen, the sounds slowly tapering.

Sometime in the night of delicious sleep, he stirred, vaguely aware that a woman—some woman—had opened the door to the room, looked down on him and then softly closed the door again. Too drowsy to think, it seemed a warm and pleasant, if unexpected, occurrence. For a moment, he wondered who it was and why. In a moment more, he was breathing slowly and rhythmically, sleeping deeply once again.

Chapter Fourteen

With one horse pulling the rented buckboard and two others tied behind, Matt was at the reins, trying to guide it over smooth ground, avoiding ruts and stones. When, at last, he found a level path, he asked, "Was that you in the night, Miss Betty?"

The woman beside him took her eyes off Tom who lay sleeping in the back of the swaying wagon. Her smile was quick and a bit self-conscious. "Could've been," she admitted. "Truth is, I wanted to be sure that Wanda hadn't come sneaking back in there." She laughed at the thought. "That old girl thought you were mighty pretty."

Matt felt a flush start at the back of his neck and changed the subject, rolling his head to indicate Tom. "How's he doing?"

"Resting fine," Betty told him, looking again at the prone figure. "He's not got any fever and that's a good sign. Just lost enough blood to slow him down for a few days."

"You going to stay with him for a while?"

She nodded. "No offense, but . . . I think a woman can keep a place cleaner than a pair of men." She shook her head at the thought. "Can't let no infection get started. I gotta keep fresh bandages on his side, wash the wound and keep it clean every day."

"You all said it wasn't a bad wound," Matt reminded her.

"Well, it's not. Not as bad as lots. Didn't hit anything vital. Still, you don't want to mess around if you got a hole that size in you."

"Why didn't you keep him in town," Matt asked, "where he could get doctoring if he needed it?"

" 'Cause he'd be up and down at the bar, drinking and telling everybody that the whiskey was curing him from the inside out," she said vehemently. " 'Cause he'd not get a lick of rest trying to rollick with the girls. And 'cause of that Dutch Snyder. That sonofabitch would love to catch Tom with his dobbers down." With a swift, angry motion, she reached to the floor of the wagon for a tiny stone and hurled it at the rump of the horse, startling it forward with a lurch.

The buckboard bounced before Matt could rein in and, from the wagonbed, Tom gave a small moan of discomfort.

"He'll be better off at the ranch," the young woman declared with a guilty glance at Tom. She reached out a comforting hand to pat Tom's shoulder. "We'll keep him down and keep him quiet."

"Like hell," came Tom's husky voice. He gave a wheezing grunt as he lifted himself up on one elbow and twisted his head to look at them. "If you don't shake me to death taking me home, I guess I'll survive having nothing to eat till when we get there."

"Hungry," Betty said with a chuckle. "That's a good sign."

"We about there?" Tom asked, straining to look around. "Damn!" he swore as he touched his side and lowered himself back down onto the pad of blankets.

"Another twenty minutes," Matt assured him. "You just lie back and take it easy."

"You take 'er easy," Tom growled, "and see if you can't miss a couple of them chuckholes."

When they reached the ranch house, they eased Tom out of the wagon and helped him inside and onto his bed. Looking pale, he was not at all argumentative about it.

"Still want something to eat?" Betty asked doubtfully.

"Maybe after I lay down fer awhile," he said in a tired response. "Maybe some soup if you could fix it . . . if you don't think it'd run out the hole in my side."

She came from the bedroom as Matt returned from the barn. "Fell asleep," she said softly, cautioning him to move quietly, "just while I was talking to him." She moved into the kitchen, opening cupboard drawers, finally finding the big iron pot she was searching for. "He wants soup and I'll make some if he's got the fixings." She nodded to the bedroom. "He'll likely sleep till suppertime."

"What can I do?"

"You might lift that trapdoor under the rug there in

the pantry," she instructed. "Go on down to the cellar and see if there's any potatoes left that he ain't let spoil. There's a candle just inside the opening."

Matt nodded and headed for the pantry. He pulled back the rug and opened the trapdoor in the floor. He peered into the dark hole, looked for and found the candle and matches. He lit the candle and descended a short ladder into the cellar.

The flickering candlelight revealed a fairly large underground chamber lined by earthen walls with frosted lower layers. Through the brief high country summer, the cellar retained the mountain winter temperature. It was cold, almost an icehouse. A rickety stand of shelves supported some salted wild game meat, a variety of canned vegetables, and a dozen rotten apples laid in a row next to a second row of potatoes. Matt inspected them one by one, finding only one or two that looked questionable. He tossed the suspect spuds into an empty apple basket and swept the rotten apples into it as well. He took a sack from the shelf, filled it with the remaining potatoes and carried them to the opening. "Potatoes look all right," he called as he took two steps up the ladder, lifting the sack to the floor above. "Bringing out some bad apples."

Betty reached down to help as he lifted the basket. She made a face at the sight and smell. "Lordy, this man!"

Matt took a last look around at the cellar before extinguishing the candle, climbed up and closed the trapdoor. He walked out of the pantry into the kitchen. "Anything else?"

"Just keep outta my way," she told him with a grin.

* * *

In an hour, she joined him in the swing on the porch. "He's still asleep," she told him. "Soup's simmering." She gave a push with her legs, starting the swing into a gentle motion. "That no-account Snyder. Hiding out whenever trouble comes. What a coward!" With a nod of her head, she turned her anger toward Tom's bedroom. "He shouldn't have gone against the two of them by himself," she said matter-of-factly. "Somebody should've stood up with him."

"Meaning me?" Matt said guiltily.

She laughed, a pleasant sound, then placed her hand upon his in a reassuring manner. "Lord, no, not you, boy." She shook her head at the thought. "You ain't no gunfighter and it wasn't your affair. Nathan or Joe Calvecci could've put a rifle on that Varney fellow and kept him out of it."

Matt made a face.

"You'd likely do it the next time," she said, guessing his thoughts. "You'd know what to do."

"But *this* time he could've been killed," Matt said solemnly. "And he's not in all that good shape as it is."

"He'll be all right," she assured him. Nonetheless, she cast an anxious glance into the ranch house. "He does looks a little feverish."

"Infection?" Matt asked.

She gave an uneasy shake of her head. "Hope not. That Chinaman dobbed him up as clean as could be. Still, it might be festering a bit inside."

"Anything we can do?" Matt asked.

"Keep him down. Make him rest."

They sat in silence, swinging to and fro.

"Tell me about yourself, Matt," she said. "You got a girl back there in Nebraska City?"

Matt smiled and gave a little chuckle. "Sort of."

"Sort of?"

"Well, I think so," he said. "There's a new family come to town. They got a daughter that's . . . well, we've talked a bit and we've being seeing each other."

"What's her name?"

"Elizabeth," Matt told her. "Elizabeth Carpenter."

"You call her Lizzie?"

Matt laughed. "Not if I value my health. I'd be better off calling out Jack Moss than to call her Lizzie."

"So what is it? Beth?"

Matt nodded. "Yes, she prefers that."

"Serious between you two?"

"It could've been, I expect," Matt responded in a regretful voice. "But this shooting thing came up and, well, I've been kind of keeping my distance . . . and having her do the same."

"Why in the world?"

"Well, you know if Jack Moss would happen to find me while we were together, she might get hurt." He paused, then added, "I think her parents might feel that way too. They're very protective of her."

"Nice people?"

"Very nice. Respectable folks."

Again, there was silence.

"I guess you're getting up the nerve to ask me, aren't you?" Betty asked unexpectedly.

"Ask what?"

"Ask me how and why I got to be a whore," she said, her candor surprising and embarrassing Matt.

"I wasn't—"

"Well, if you weren't, you'd be one of the few," she interrupted. "*My* folks were poor and trash at that," she told him, her face grave and frowning as she remembered. "Lived in a little town in Kentucky where nobody decent would have anything to do with us. Pa drank all the time and my ma did too. Couple of brothers that was always in trouble." She paused, her mind replaying her childhood. "I ran away when I was fifteen 'cause I thought that anything would be better than staying there. Town boys thought they could do whatever they pleased with me." She gave Matt a pretty smile. "Even whoring was better than it would've been if I'd stayed."

"I wasn't going to ask," Matt protested.

Betty gave a short laugh. "Well, then, maybe it's just that I wanted to tell you. You see, there's nothing any of us want more than to somehow, someway, get enough money ahead to where we can live someplace nice and be respectable." She turned her face to him, her eyes misty. "Can someone like you understand that?"

"I guess so," Matt said awkwardly. "I guess I never thought about. . . ." He stopped in embarrassment.

"Saloon whores?" Betty supplied the words. "Just poor girls, mainly," she continued. "Some like the life, but most only want a home and a husband just like anybody else."

"And you picked somebody like Patterson?"

"I 'spect you're right," she agreed, nodding at his

cynicism. "If I was a smart and scheming woman, Tom would be the last I'd favor." She slowly shook her head. "Tom just kinda happened. He drinks too much and, God knows, he can be mean when he needs to, but he was always gallant to me." She glanced toward the house, a soft and loving look on her face. "Lots of men try to flatter you when they want you upstairs, but Tom was never like that. He made me out to be special and, you could tell, he thought I was."

"Miss Betty," Matt began hesitantly, not sure that he should say anything at all, "he's a man who kills people and a drunk that can't stop drinking. What kind of a life would you have if you settled for him?"

"I don't know that I have," Betty replied evenly. "I guess I'll have to make up my mind pretty soon." She touched the wound at the side of her face. "Even if I don't get scarred up by some scalawag, I'll lose my looks anyway." She gazed off at the mountains. "Calvecci might marry me."

Matt looked at her in surprise. "That's not what you'd want, is it?"

She laughed, shedding her anguish in a rush of good humor. "My God, Matt, if I wasn't too old and such a goodhearted woman, I'd set my cap for you."

Her merriment was infectious and Matt joined her in laughter, somehow flattered even though he recognized the comment as jest.

She rose from the swing and turned toward the house. "I 'spect that soup ought to be simmered enough for a meal. You want something a little more filling?"

"Soup will be fine," Matt agreed, rising to walk with

her, opening the door for her to enter. "Will you need some help with him?"

"No," she answered. "I'm a strong woman."

"Indeed you are," Matt said sincerely.

Tom Patterson's fever rose near midnight and, through the rest of the night and the following day Betty and Matt took turns applying cooling towels and giving sponge baths. Betty prepared and applied a warm bread poultice to the wound to draw out the infection and fed him spoonfuls of an opiate concoction the Chinese barber had sent along in case of need. At times, he sat up in bed, delirious in his speech, staring hard at the nightmares of his past, then collapsing back into his shivering stupors.

Near the dawning of the following morning, the fever broke and Tom slept peacefully. Coming into the room, Betty gave Matt a tired smile and waved him out of the room. "You get some sleep, you've been with him most of the night."

"So have you."

She nodded. "That's all right. I can sleep just as well right here in my chair as laying down. You go on."

"Wake me if you need me."

"Go on, he's doing just fine now."

Chapter Fifteen

At noon, Matt came out of his exhausted sleep with a sense of urgency. For an unfathomed reason and still needing hours more rest, he was now fully alert. He hurried into his trousers and, tucking in his shirt, entered the main room of the cabin and was not surprised to see Betty at the window.

"Who's coming?" Matt asked.

"Dutch Snyder," she said almost in a whisper. "Several others riding with him."

Matt took a look toward Tom's bedroom.

"He's still out," Betty told him. "I couldn't wake him." She gave Matt a reassuring smile. "He's better. Much better."

Matt nodded and took a step toward the door.

"Take the rifle, Matt," Betty cautioned.

Matt frowned, watching the riders coming closer. "I think they'd make that a reason to shoot, Betty."

"That's a mistake," Betty said, looking for the Henry. She saw it in a corner and went after it.

Matt walked out onto the porch to await the arrival of the riders while Betty stayed just inside the front door.

Dutch Snyder and four others, a scruffy lot with their guns drawn, thundered up to the house, reining up their horses as they saw Matt on the porch.

"Is Tom Patterson in there?" Snyder asked.

"He's here," Matt answered evenly. "He's in no shape to be disturbed."

"We heard he was gutshot," said a pockmarked miner.

"That's probably why you took the chance of coming out here," Matt said "What do you want?"

"Keep your eyes on the doors," Snyder instructed his men. He swung down from his horse and pulled a rifle from the saddle holster as he turned toward Matt. "This is official, boy," he said. He waved at the men behind him, a couple of miners who looked uncomfortable on horseback and two surly cowhands. "These men are duly deputized by me and we're here to put Tom Patterson under arrest for murder."

"Murder?" Matt questioned. "For what happened in town?"

"Cold-blooded murder they tell me," Snyder said righteously.

"Maybe if you'd stayed in town, you'd know better," Matt countered.

The retort angered Snyder and, as he'd done before with his baton at the saloon, he punched the rifle muzzle against Matt's chest with considerable force, the repeated jabs backing the young man across the porch. "Stand aside. You're interfering with the law."

The pockmarked miner laughed. "Better do what he says, boy!"

Betty stepped from the doorway with the Henry aimed at Snyder. "Stay outta here, Snyder," she said, her voice husky and tremulous. "You and your bunch clear out."

Snyder smiled at the sight of her and turned to his followers. "Well, we got a pantywaist kid and a saloon whore to deal with," he said. "Ain't you all scared?"

"That *lady* will take your head off, Snyder," came a voice from a new quarter, causing heads to swivel in alarm. "If she don't, I will."

Ridiculous in appearance, a gaunt apparition, Tom stood in his sweat-soaked BVD's at the back end of the ranch house, rock steady and forbidding in his outrage, a revolver in each hand. "Guns on the ground. Do it now!"

Fearfully, the men threw down their rifles and sidearms.

"You too, Snyder," Tom instructed.

"This'll go hard on you, Patterson!" Snyder blustered. "You're resisting arrest—"

"Damned right I am! Now, drop that rifle or I'll drop you."

Snyder let the rifle fall from his hands.

Matt bent down to pick it up. "I'm getting just a little sore in the chest," he said to Snyder. He thrust the rifle muzzle into Snyder's belly with a sharp poke, doubling the heavy man over with a gasp. He waited until

Snyder caught his breath, then slammed the barrel below his left kneecap. Snyder howled and fell to the ground and grabbed for his knee, holding it to him as he rolled in acute misery in the dirt. "That kinda hurts, doesn't it, *Marshal*?" Matt said. He walked behind the agonized man and prodded the barrel repeatedly to the fallen man's rear, each sharp jab bringing the Snyder up to his one good knee, scrambling to get away from the torment. "Maybe this'll help speed you along your way."

Snyder scuttled across the ground and struggled to his feet behind his horse, hobbling to hide behind it as Tom, Betty, and Matt gave way to their laughter. Two of the men on horseback snickered, then brayed in loud guffaws.

"Maybe you'll get your guns back when we feel fit to come into town," Tom chuckled. "Try not to rile any mountain cats or grizzlies on your way home."

Snyder glared, furious at them all. Hardly able to bend his sore leg up to the stirrup, he finally managed to hoist himself up, then flinched as his abused bottom touched the saddle. "You'll pay for this," he bellowed, "all of you!"

Tom fired a shot past his ear, close enough that the fleshy man ducked and whipped his horse away to a frantic pace, his duly deputized followers in distressed pursuit.

Betty, Tom, and Matt cackled anew at the sight of Dutch Snyder standing as tall in his saddle as he could on his one good leg, trying to avoid the bounce beneath his aching rump as they raced across the mountain meadow.

"Who-o-o-e-e!" Tom exclaimed as he staggered through an impromptu jig of joy. "That was worth pulling out that Chinaman's stitches!"

"Let's get you back in bed, you old rooster!" Betty cried, her laughter still bubbling. "Come on, Matt," she instructed, leading him in a rush. "Get him before he falls in a swoon!"

One on either side, they helped him toward the ranch house.

"How'd you get out there?" Matt asked.

"Went through the window," Tom replied, shuffling between them, his hand holding his side. "Couldn't bend and couldn't straighten up, but, somehow, I got out of her."

"You probably tore out something for sure," Betty tried to scold him over her merriment. "Didja see what Matt did to *Marshal* Snyder?"

"Lordy, yes," Tom chuckled. "Boy, you done made yourself another enemy. He'll not likely live that down as long as he stays in these parts." He shook his head, sobering. "He'll try to get even."

"I'd rather look forward to that," Matt responded, immediately appearing apologetic for his bravado.

Tom and Betty looked at him in astonishment and broke into laughter once again.

"Damned if I don't believe you would," Tom chortled.

Tom stayed in bed for the rest of the day and the morning of the next. At lunch, he hobbled out of the bedroom, bent over to ease the hurt in his side.

"Well, look at Mr. Patterson!" Betty announced with

pleasure. "Come back to life and ready for his noonday meal."

"No more damned soup," Tom muttered, glancing down at the table, his eyes riveted upon the venison steak on Matt's plate. "You got another of them?"

"Fry you one soon as you sit down," Betty told him, pulling out a chair for him. "Be back in a minute."

She left the kitchen for a moment, then returned with a butcher-wrapped package. She took a sizable cut of meat from the package and put it on a hot skillet, the moist steak hissing loudly.

"How are you doing, boy?" Tom asked.

"Fine, Tom," Matt replied.

"Done any practicing?"

Matt shook his head. "We kinda thought it'd be too much noise."

"Hell, it wouldn't have bothered me," Tom grumbled. "You ought to get back at it. Right now."

"Can I finish lunch first?" Matt asked with a smile.

"Still going to shoot like a girl?"

"Whatever gets the job done," Matt answered, cutting a piece of steak and putting it into his mouth.

Tom turned to Betty, jerking his left thumb at Matt. "You know what he's doing? Using two hands to hold up a pistol." He shook his head in disgust. "I never saw nothing like it."

Betty turned the steak on the skillet, the sound of frying almost louder than her response. "Does it help him?"

"I can hit what I'm aiming at," Matt said, cutting off any comment from Tom.

"Then, it ought to be all right," Betty said. "Matt shouldn't have to worry about that Jack Moss anyhow." She poked the steak with a fork, stabbing it with intensity. "Ought to be some lawmen here in the territory to put scum like him in jail where they can't bother decent folks."

"Lawmen like Dutch Snyder?" Tom asked, a sly smile on his face.

She made a face, lifting the steak out and onto a plate with a fork. "Here you go."

"Is it well done?" Tom asked, suspicious. "Wasn't on there more than a couple of minutes."

With a sigh, Betty flipped the steak back onto the skillet.

"What are you going to do about Snyder's charges?" Matt asked.

Tom yawned. "Nothing."

"Just that easy?" Matt persisted. "Just ignore a murder charge?"

"Hell," Tom swore, "I got outstanding warrants on me in other places in the country . . . better ones than what I done in Gold Stream." He looked anxiously to the steak. "Get her done on both sides," he said crossly and turned back to Matt. "He came after me this time 'cause he know'd I was laid up. He ain't going to try it again any time soon." He turned to Betty, irritation on his face. "Don't I get any coffee?"

"Make it yourself," she declared peevishly, then turned to Matt. "The old fool must be getting well! He ain't fit company, like a bear with a sore paw."

"What in 'tarnation has got into you?" Tom asked her. "I get outta bed for the first damned time—"

"And don't you *dare* ask me for any whiskey!" She pointed an accusing finger at him. "You touch a drop and I'll go back to town quicker than a wink."

Without waiting for a response, she marched out of the kitchen, leaving the steak sizzling on the stove.

"What's wrong with her?" Tom asked, mystified.

"You want your steak?" Matt asked, rising to walk to the stove.

"Yeah, don't want 'er fried too hard," Tom responded. "What's wrong with Betty?"

Matt put the steak on the plate and handed it to the older man. "I think she cares about you."

"Got a funny way of showing it," Tom said, cutting the steak. "Maybe she's wore out looking after us."

"Looking after you," Matt corrected him. "You're the one who's causing grief."

"You mean me fussing at her?" Tom asked.

"Yeah, that, getting infected and running a fever, crawling out windows, fighting with the so-called law," Matt said, returning to his seat to resume eating. "And then, there's the drinking."

"Never mind about the drinking," Tom snapped. "That ain't none of your concern or hers."

"You're right about that," Matt replied, chewing as he spoke. "Man not strong enough to drink sensible ought not to be of any concern to anybody."

"Open your mouth once more—"

"Seems like everybody wants to say that to me," Matt cut in. He finished the steak on his plate, rose, and walked to the door, sweeping his gun belt from the peg.

"Where you heading?" Tom asked.

"I'd better get out of the house and start practicing," Matt told him. "Like Betty said, you ain't fit company now that you're getting well."

Chapter Sixteen

For the rest of the day and the following morning, the rout of Dutch Snyder and his ragtag posse continued as the subject of their conversations.

"Didja see him tiptoeing up in them stirrups?" Tom whooped in laughter, the convulsion causing pain in his side, sobering him to a grim chuckle. "Gutless sonofabitch!"

"Still pretty sore?" Matt asked, a glance to Betty to share her concern.

Tom caught the glance and grumbled his displeasure. "I've had worse."

"You ain't got many lives left, you old tomcat," Betty chided him. "Crawling out that window could've opened you up again."

Tom lifted his shirt to peer at the angry red weal beneath his ribs. "Looks just fine to me."

They were sitting at the kitchen table late into the

morning, once more reliving Matt's confrontation of Snyder and his so-called posse.

"Don't take Snyder too lightly," Betty warned. "He ain't gonna mess with Tom 'lessen he's too drunk or too shot up to matter, but he'll figure that you're a different sort."

"That ain't necessarily so," Tom chuckled. "Not after Matt goosed him back to town." He gave a wave toward Matt. "I'd say this boy is man enough to take care of himself in a fight."

"Who says it would be a fair fight?" Betty countered, arching her eyebrows at Matt. "Mind my word and stay clear of him."

"Dutch won't last too long," Tom advised them. "Some rowdy will run him off and then they'll have somebody better or somebody worse."

Betty rose from the table to clear the cups.

"One of these days," Tom continued. "They'll do the papers to make Gold Stream into a real town if the mining company comes in and the ore don't play out."

Betty turned to give them a cheerless smile. "If it does, then Gold Stream will just dry up and blow away and we'll all be gone."

"Ghost town?" Matt ventured the question.

Tom nodded. "Ain't much of a reason for the place if there ain't no gold or silver to be had. Pretty tough high country to the west and no easy pass to get through."

"Ranching?" Matt asked.

"It's better down in South Park. That's where I'd head if I didn't have my place here. Winters get mighty cold up here."

"We got company again," Betty announced, moving to the side door. "Charlie Meacham, I think."

Tom rose from the table and joined her, looking out at the approaching rider. "Now what?" he grumbled. "I sure ain't in no condition to come at Calvecci's beck and call."

Tom, Betty, and Matt moved out into the yard to wait at the fence for the elderly man to arrive. Meacham spurred his horse into a trot, waving an envelope. "Gotta letter here for young Mr. Matt," he shouted. "Got *Urgent* printed on its outsides they tells me!"

Matt stepped forward as the old man reined his horse to a halt, then reached up to take the envelope.

"Come this morning on the stage down at the freight station," the old man told them. "Relayed from Nebraska City through Denver and then up to Gold Stream."

Matt opened the envelope and unfolded the letter.

"Your pa?" Betty asked.

Matt shook his head. "From the sheriff in Nebraska City." He began reading, his face sober as he scanned the signature. His eyes began to glisten, tears welling as he read the letter. "Dad's dead," he said huskily, passing the letter to Tom as he walked away quickly, striding into the ranch house.

Tom looked at the letter, studied it for a moment without comprehension, then handed it to Betty in some embarrassment. "Maybe you can make her out?"

Betty looked at the note for a long time, struggling to read it. "It's addressed to Matt," she began, "from the sheriff there at Nebraska City." Betty paused with a grimace, her eyes meeting Tom's with dismay before returning to the letter. "He says here that they found Matt's father all cut up and killed by somebody. They don't say who."

"Don't need to. Sonofabitching Jack Moss," Tom growled. "Worked the old man over to find out where the boy would be."

"Do you think he'd have told him?" Betty questioned anxiously. "I don't know that—"

"Sure, he'd have told," Tom interrupted. "He wouldn't have wanted to, but Jack would've stayed at him till hell freezes over to make him talk." He turned and looked out at the horizon, directing his anger to the vicious enemy wherever he might be. "Sonofabitching Jack Moss."

By midday, Matt was packed and ready to ride, his horse saddled and waiting, Tom and Betty standing beside him at the hitching rail.

"Your dad wouldn't think this is the right thing to do," Betty said, anxiety in her voice. "Stay with us."

Tom nodded in agreement. "The burying is most likely already done and there's no cause to go back to Nebraska City. Hell, Jack Moss will be figgering that's just what you'll do."

"There's the store to take care of," Matt said somberly.

"You didn't seem too keen on running that store when you first showed up," Tom reminded him. "Selling out might be a good idea. Take the money and get yourself outta the territory, back East somewhere."

"That was then," Matt told him. "It isn't really the store. It's what Jack Moss has done to us. If I'd been home, Dad wouldn't have died." He paused, then declared, "I won't run again."

"You didn't run the first time," Tom argued. "Your pa know'd you couldn't go against a man like Moss, damned few of us can. He tried to buy you some time, to get you ready—"

"Am I really ready, Tom?" Matt interrupted. "Ready to face Jack Moss?"

Tom didn't answer for a few moments. "I don't know, Matt."

"Well, we've gone about as far as we can go, haven't we?" Matt said. "I can't go on hiding."

"Just hold on a couple more days," Tom appealed. "Till I get my strength back and I can ride with you."

Matt reached out to lay a hand on the older man's shoulder, a gesture of some affection. "You've done your best to teach me."

Tom pointed to the holstered Colt Lightning on Matt's hip. "Must not have done too good a job. You're still carrying that little popgun!"

Matt laughed and unfastened a flap of his saddlebag and brought out the Walker. "I'll take this with me if you don't mind. I don't think you approve of the way I use it, but I might just have a chance. If I do, it'll be because of you." He tucked the heavy weapon back inside, then turned to Betty. "Take good care of him, Betty. I'll get back whenever I can." He unfastened the reins and mounted his horse. "I'll get you the rest of your money, Tom," he said. "I'll be sending it on to you just as soon as I get back to Nebraska City."

"No need," Tom protested. "I've been paid plenty enough."

"A deal is a deal, Mr. Patterson," Matt declared, consciously imitating his father. "Dad would've insisted on it and so do I." He tugged the reins to the right, turning the horse away. "I'd better be on my way."

"Ride wide around Gold Stream, Matt!" Betty called. "No sense in giving Dutch Snyder a chance at you!"

"And keep your eyes open for Jack Moss!" Tom warned. "Wouldn't surprise me if you'd meet him coming in this direction!"

"Good advice! I'll try to stay off the main trail!" Matt called back, spurring the roan into a canter, waving once again.

Tom and Betty watched until he disappeared from sight.

"Think we'll ever see him again?" Betty asked. "Or know what happens to him?"

"Give me a few more days," Tom replied. "I'll ride on over to Nebraska City and see what I might be able to do."

Chapter Seventeen

Matt reined up at the sight of Gold Stream ahead. He pondered the best route to skirt the town. A ride to his left through open country would expose him almost as much as a trot down the center of town. To his right, across a stretch of flat land, a long line of aspen followed the stream, trees that could provide cover for a horse and rider. He spurred the roan and headed for the aspen.

As he rode, he could make out the activities in the mining camp, dray wagons and buckboards rolling up dust on the central lane of the town, a mule train arriving at the freight office, men on horseback, tiny figures moving to and from the faraway buildings and tents. He spurred his horse into a gallop through the sagebrush, figuring that if he could see them, they could see him as well.

He crossed the open space in a couple of minutes, slowed the horse to a walk and entered the shadows of the aspen. For the most part, he let the horse find its way through the thicket of trees, only occasionally guiding his mount. He rode deep through the woods, unable to see the town, relying upon his senses to tell him when to turn back to the left to come out well past the east end of Gold Stream.

As he turned the roan out of the trees, he glanced to the west, gratified to see Gold Stream was now a good distance behind him.

A cluster of six horsemen led by Dutch Snyder emerged from the aspen forest. They circled him quickly, guns drawn and leveled at him.

"Figgered you'd be coming today," Snyder exulted as he rode up to Matt. "We know'd that Charlie Meacham had brought you that letter and we figgered you'd be heading out for home." He gestured to the trees. "Hell, we was watching for you and saw you crossing the flats at the other end of town and figgered you'd be coming out right about here." He smiled at his own cleverness.

"Let me pass, Snyder," Matt said evenly, recognizing some of the men who'd ridden with Snyder before. "I'm leaving town."

"Not without settling a score with me," Snyder shot back.

"You're pretty brave with six others to back you," Matt said, regretting the retort immediately.

"You looking for a even-up fight?" Snyder asked, his eyes looking Matt up and down, a smirk of contempt on his face.

"I'm not looking for any fight at all," Matt replied. "Now, if you'll let me go on my way—"

"Get off your horse," Snyder commanded. He swung his heavy bulk down from his mount and handed the reins to the rider beside him. "Come on down, boy," he said with a motioning gesture. "I'll give you a fair fight with these boys as judges." He looked around at his cronies. "You'll see to it that it's fair, won't you, Bill?"

There were hoots of laughter and bellows of excitement.

"Fair and square it'll be!" shouted Bill, the pock-marked miner who had accompanied Snyder to the ranch. "Get down and get your dukes up and have at 'er!"

Behind Matt, one of the men rode in close. He reached out to snatch the revolver from Matt's holster with one hand, shoving hard with the other, slamming him out of the saddle. Matt fell to the ground heavily, the impact jolting him and knocking the wind from him.

"Get up, boy," Snyder taunted. "Let's see what you are without Tom Patterson's gun behind you." He moved forward quickly and swung his fist as Matt tried to stand up. The tremendous blow caught Matt full on the side of his face and knocked him under the hooves of his own shying horse. Barely conscious, he curled into a ball to shield his head and face from the prancing hooves, feeling one graze his head as he rolled away. He looked around wildly for Snyder, trying to find him when he felt the kick in his side and a stab of pain that galvanized him up into a protective crouch. He tried to move away to clear his head.

Snyder smiled in satisfaction and came after him, swinging another haymaker.

Matt staggered back, barely moving his head in time to avoid another smashing blow. He kept moving backward, stumbling, trying to keep distance between himself and the stalking bully.

Seeing that Matt was recovering, Snyder feinted one way, then rushed the other, swinging his massive fist.

Unexpectedly, and with a boxer's skill, Matt stepped inside the arc of Snyder's swing and jabbed a left fist to the chin of his burly antagonist. The quick thrust jolted the big man, surprising him. A second and third jab knocked him back into the center of the circle of riders.

"Lookit the fancy-dancy stuff!" the pockmarked man sneered. "Don't you know how to fight like a man?"

Angered anew, Snyder gathered himself for another rush.

Matt gave him no chance to advance. He moved in, following the advantage of his attack by stabbing short, solid blows into Snyder, staggering him.

Roaring with fury, Snyder tried to fight back, swinging wildly with his heavy arms, aiming powerhouse blows that never quite found their mark. Each time, Matt either stepped quickly out of reach or moved inside to punish Snyder with a flurry of left and right punches.

"Goddamn it, Dutch!" one of the miners shouted. "Don't let him do that to you! Knock his head off!"

"Stand still, you sonofabitch!" Snyder growled as he lumbered forward.

As Matt stepped nimbly away, another of the men reached down from his horse to grab a fistful of Matt's hair, painfully distracting and momentarily immobilizing him.

Dutch Snyder rushed forward, took aim, and swung a fearful roundhouse, but Matt tore away, catching the blow on his shoulder.

Matt backed away, circling Snyder, trying to watch those behind him as well as the brawny marshal who shuffled and lunged after him. Matt kept him away with sharp, stinging jabs to the big man's face, and solid thrusts to his middle. He moved in and out, punishing the man each time. Snyder was wheezing and moving slower now, unaccustomed to such effort and feeling the cumulative effects of the punches. He repeatedly shook his head, trying to clear it, pawing at Matt, trying to grapple with him. Matt avoided each grasping lunge, flicking jabs to Snyder's face, continually circling and tiring the big man out as he attempted to close in. Finally, Matt stepped away, knowing that Snyder was almost finished and now turned his attention to the others that surrounded him. *What to do about them? Will they let me go?*

Snyder then surprised him with a sweeping right, a heavy blow that knocked Matt to his knees. Before he could recover, Snyder was behind him, the weight of his heavy body thrust against the small of Matt's back, a brawny arm around his neck straining to bend him back, trying to break his back.

Matt summoned all his strength to twist slightly to the side, stretched his left arm out straight for a moment, then slamming his left elbow back into his tormentor's stomach. He felt the big man flinch and the hold on his neck lessen slightly. Again and again, Matt drove his elbow into the man's soft belly, twisting to loosen the hold.

He broke free and scrambled away, getting some distance from him. Snyder made a half-hearted effort to pursue but he was panting, bending down, one hand moving down to his belly to massage the pain in his gut. He paused to take a deep breath, trying to recover.

Matt moved without hesitation, winding up a right uppercut with as much strength as he had left and smashing his fist on the point of Snyder's chin.

Cupping his right hand with his left to assuage the pain, Matt stepped away and watched as Snyder stood dazed, unable to move or function. With disregard for the pain, Matt swung again, a final blow that toppled the big man to the ground where he lay still.

Breathing hard, he turned to direct his gaze to the pockmarked man, selecting him as his next possible adversary. "You promised me a fair fight."

The miner looked down at his fallen leader, disbelief on his blemished face. He turned his gaze to the other men, then looked down on Matt, a smile showing stained and rotten teeth. "We take it back," he said. "Didn't mean a word of it."

Matt glanced from man to man, wondering who would make the first move. He returned his gaze to the pockmarked man. "Whatever you plan to do," he said, his breath coming raggedly, "don't forget about Tom Patterson."

The miner couldn't hide his look of concern. "What do you mean?"

"I'll fight my own battles," Matt said, getting stronger, "and I'll warn you right here . . . if you don't kill me, I'll come after each man that lays a hand on me." He paused, watching them carefully. "And if you do kill me, Tom Patterson will make it right for me. He'll not leave any one of you alive."

The men sat in their horses in silence, the threat obviously making an impression.

"Let me go right now," Matt persisted, turning to sweep his gaze across each man, recognizing the indecision in each face. "This was between Snyder and me. . . ."

Too late, he heard the movement behind him. He started to turn just in time to see Dutch Snyder swing the heavy baton. Matt threw up an arm to partially deflect the blow as he ducked away. Nonetheless, the hickory rod slammed against his head causing an explosion of pain and blinding light, then oblivion.

Dutch Snyder looked down on Matt, wanting to inflict additional punishment, but too beaten and weary to swing the club again. Exhausted, he handed the baton back to his henchman. "Thanks, Bill," he wheezed. "Somebody put him on his horse and take him up to the jail. I'll take care of him later."

Chapter Eighteen

Betty stirred in her sleep, disturbed by a frightening sound; something dreadful penetrated her dreams and brought her awake with a start.

Tom was not in the bed with her.

She listened carefully, something from her nightmare persisting into the reality of the dark night, an undefined terror that brought a pounding to her heart.

She rose from the bed, put on her wrapper, stepped into her slippers and hurried into the living room.

Then, she froze, hearing the sound clearly: terrible screams of pain, not human, and wails of unendurable agony. She saw the flickering reflections of flame on the walls of the room and, in horror, ran for the side door.

Tom reached out of the darkness and pulled her to him. He was half-dressed, in jeans and boots, with six-guns in the holsters at his hip and a rifle in his hands.

"It's too late, Bett," he whispered to her, his voice

ragged with rage and despair. "They've fired the barn."

"The horses!" she cried. "They'll—"

"They're burning to death," Tom cut in harshly, his voice almost lost in the keening, high whinnies of torment knifing through the night. "We can't get to them."

Suddenly, there was a sharp report, followed by another and the horrible sounds stopped.

"Thank God," Tom said heavily.

"What was that?" Betty exclaimed, confused and terrified.

"Somebody shot 'em," Tom said. "Guess there's somebody out there who might have some sort of a heart."

"Who, Tom?" Betty demanded. "What's happening?"

"Reckon we'll find out soon," he replied. "I can see 'em out there in the firelight."

Betty looked out into the yard, the light from the burning barn now brightening the area. In the shadows, fifty or sixty feet from the house, she, too, could see dark silhouettes of men on horseback, moving back and forth.

"Tom Patterson!" came a call in a loud, brusque voice. "Come on out!"

"Who are they?" Betty said in fright.

"Jack Moss and his bunch, I reckon," Tom said, his voice dropping to a husky whisper. "I shoulda heard 'em early on."

"You coming out, Tom?" a shout demanded.

Tom stepped to the side door, staying behind the heavy logs of the walls. "It's Jack Moss, ain't it?"

"Funny kind of a get-together, Tom!" the man shouted. "Never thought you and I'd be having a problem."

"What's the problem, Jack?"

"You got that McKay whelp in there!" came the response. "Heard from his old man that you were helping out, showing him how to go against me!"

"I 'spect Mr. McKay didn't volunteer that information!" Tom countered.

"We're wasting time, Tom! Send him out and I'll forget about your part in it!"

"There ain't nobody to send out, Jack!" Tom responded. "Young McKay's long gone, probably back in Nebraska City by now!"

"Well, we'll know that once you come on out of there, won't we?"

"Don't figure on coming out under a bunch of guns, Jack! I'd be pretty stupid to do that, now wouldn't I?"

"Be a lot smarter than staying in that house, Tom!" Moss said, a light laugh in his voice. "Things might get a little hot for you!"

"My God," Betty said, her voice strong with terror. "He's going to burn us alive!"

"Get down low," Tom commanded. "Over there, behind the table."

Betty looked at him, fear immobilizing her.

"Get down," Tom said with a softer urgency. "There's going to be bullets flying through here any minute."

Betty nodded and sought shelter on the floor beneath the heavy oak table.

"There *is* somebody in there!" Moss shouted. "I heard 'em!"

"Ain't no boy in here!" Tom responded. "Just me and a woman, that's all!"

"Well, then, come on out like I said and we'll

know!" Moss persisted. "We ain't going to hurt you all if you do!"

"Anybody who'd burn horses ain't to be trusted!" Tom said scathingly. "I do want to thank whoever it was that put 'em out of their misery . . . all of you ain't complete bastards!"

"Last chance, Tom! Send the boy out!"

"I'm telling you there ain't no boy!" Tom shouted and stepped closer to the doorway, steadying his rifle against the doorframe, taking aim into the fire-flickering shadows. "Ride out and leave us alone!"

A shot exploded into the wall, followed by a volley from other guns, bullets crashing through the windows and the door into the living room. Dishes in the kitchen were shattered, cans blasted from shelves, and the bullets ricocheted through the cabin.

Tom fired into the shadows and had the satisfaction of hearing a rider cry out.

"Hope it was you, Jack!" he shouted, whirling away from the door, moving toward a front window.

The reply was another barrage into the house, most of it aimed at the doorway he'd just vacated.

"You all right?" he asked Betty.

She gave an uncertain nod.

"They're around the house," he told her. "Can't tell how many." He raised his head up to peek out the shattered window. "Six, maybe seven. Don't know whether I nicked or killed Jack or one of them others."

"Maybe if I'd go out and tell them . . ." Betty said hoarsely, unable to finish the statement. She cleared her throat. "Maybe they'd believe me that Matt's gone."

"They ain't planning to let any of us out of here alive, lady."

"Then . . . what will we do?"

"Fight 'em off as long as we can," he replied. He raised up and brought the rifle sight to his right eye and squeezed off a shot. "Be nice if you could use a gun."

Betty crept out of the darkness to the window to join him. "Give me one," she said. "I'll give it a try."

Tom handed her a revolver and showed her how to cock it. "Stay low here at the window. Just take your time and take a shot if you think you got a target."

Betty lifted the handgun gingerly, not exactly sure of her familiarity with it. She cocked it and nodded with satisfaction, then peeked over the windowsill and fired one shot, then another.

"Good girl," Tom assured her. "Pick a target and try to lead him."

He moved across the floor to the front door and dropped flat, his rifle aimed out into the flame-bright night, waiting, not firing as the thump-thump-thump of bullets slammed into the walls.

After a few minutes, the tempo of firing increased. Tom and Betty kept as low as possible, listening to the bullets as they punched and burrowed into the logs of the house. Tom glanced around, trying to listen over the sounds of the assault, his eyes moving up to the roof. "They're firing the house from the backside. Somebody got a torch up on the roof."

"We've got to give up, Tom!" Betty pleaded. "I'd rather get shot than burn to death!"

"Get into the kitchen," Tom instructed, "soon as the firing lets up next time they reload."

A few minutes later, the gunfire subsided and the hiss of fire on the roof became audible, wisps of smoke beginning to curl down from the shingles.

"Been a good old house," Tom complained as he crawled across the floor toward the kitchen. "Feller did a nice job of building her."

"What are we going to do, Tom?" Betty exclaimed in fright, crawling with him.

"I hate to lose her," Tom continued as he moved through the doorway into the kitchen, reaching out to draw Betty to him. "Only place I ever had that I could call my own."

"Damn it, Tom," she said in exasperation. "We're going to be burned alive and you're here grieving about losing this danged house."

"Maybe we will and maybe we won't," Tom replied, making a gesture toward the pantry. "You get over there and open that door down into the cellar while I keep 'em busy for a while." He crouchwalked his way to a cabinet, took out two more Colts and several boxes of ammunition.

Betty looked at him open-mouthed. "The cellar?" She pondered the possibilities, then shook her head uncertainly. "Can't the fire and smoke get down there too?"

"Hope not," he replied. "It's either go out there and get shot or stay here in this danged wooden house and take our chances. We ain't got much choice. Get on down there now."

Obediently, Betty crawled to the pantry, pulled back the rug and opened the trapdoor. She descended partway into the chamber below, pausing to light the candle, only her head still above the level of the floor, her eyes watching Tom anxiously.

He moved across the floor to the side window and peeked out into the night, the firelight from the barn brightly illuminating the house perimeter on the south end, a new glow beginning on the north. At the front of the living room, Tom could see the flames eating through the roof, a rafter burning steadily, smoke billowing, sparks and embers cascading down onto the furnishings. He slid two of the Colts across the room to Betty, followed by the boxes of ammunition. "Take them down there," he instructed. "We may be needing them later."

Betty nodded, gathering the firearms and ammunition, disappearing from view as she carried them below.

Keeping an eye on the fire's advance, Tom began firing steadily at the shadows, hoping that a few shots would find a mark.

"Come on out, Tom!" Jack Moss shouted from the darkness. "Bad way to die!"

"No way's a good way to die!" Tom shouted back, his voice hard to hear over the roar and crackle of the devouring flames. "Go to hell!"

"Looks like you're there ahead of me!" Moss yelled back, a cackle of glee rising in his voice.

Then, with a gusting storm of fire, the roof of the living room collapsed, the burning timbers tumbling down while a sheet of flame flashed across the room, flaring into the kitchen.

Tom dove to the floor and rolled toward the pantry to escape the reaching flames. Betty ducked down into the cellar and Tom came tumbling through the opening behind her, his hands reaching up to close the trapdoor, pulling it tight into the aperture. He stood for a moment, letting his eyes adjust to the light of Betty's candle, glancing around at their earthen enclosure.

"Over there," he said to Betty, pointing to a far corner of the cellar. "That part ain't under the rest of the house." He moved to a different corner, rummaged around through an old washstand and found a bundle of rags. "Here," he told her, offering her the rags. "There's a bottle of grape juice over there on the shelf. Wet these down and put 'em over your face. May help with the smoke."

"Are we going to live, Tom?"

"We got a chance, hon," he replied as he blew out the candle. "That's as much as I can say."

Jack Moss sat on his horse, his men gathered behind him, all staring in fascination at the spectacle; the blazing barn and ranch house making the night as bright as day.

"I'd have come out," one of his men said, his voice hushed. "I wouldn't have stayed."

"I'd have thought so too," Moss agreed.

"Think there was a woman in there like he said?" Bob Daly asked.

"More likely young McKay," Moss replied. "There was more than one shooting."

They waited, watching as the house collapsed, as the fire from the barn began to burn itself out.

"We staying, boss?" Bob asked.

Jack Moss didn't answer for a long while as he continued to stare at the flaming structure. Finally, he turned, his dark, bearded face, devilish in the glow from the fire. "No need, I 'spect," he said, more to himself than to his henchman. "Be a long, frosty night waiting. We might as well head into Gold Stream."

"What about Lige?" his henchman asked, gesturing to the dead man sprawled on the ground, his horse grazing beside the body. "We gonna bury him?"

"Let him lie," Moss said. "'Less you boys want to pass up some of the sporting girls there in town."

Daly shook his head. "I'll take his horse." He spurred his own mount forward and leaned out of the saddle to grasp the dangling reins of the dead man's horse, leading the mare back to join Moss.

"Been a good night," Moss said to him as he turned his horse away. "Never liked Tom Patterson. It's good to have him dead."

He spurred his horse and set off down the pass, Bob riding beside him and his men following close behind.

"Funny thing about Patterson killing poor old Lige," Bob confided.

Jack Moss turned in the saddle, waiting to hear.

"Lige was the one who had the soft heart and shot the horses," Bob chuckled. "And that's the thanks he got for it."

Moss thought that was funny, too, and they shared their laughter as they rode down the trail in the darkness.

Chapter Nineteen

When Matt came to his senses, he was disoriented. Wherever he was, it was pitch black and quiet, the air hot and stifling. His head throbbed with pain and, tenderly touching the back of it, he found a large bump that was sore as the devil. For a few minutes, he had a hard time remembering exactly what had happened, the memory of the fight almost blasted from his mind. Then, as he discovered other areas of pain, he recalled Snyder's kicks and blows and had a dim remembrance of the hickory stick swinging at his head.

He lay still for a time to let his feeling of nausea pass, then cautiously stood up and reached out his hands to explore his surroundings. A couple of steps forward brought him to a bare wall. With a slow step and patient care, he followed the wall to a corner, then to another with a door that he tried and found securely locked. On the fourth wall, he was able to discern a high, tiny window that transmitted the lighter darkness of the night outside. It seemed that he was locked in an empty room. There was no furniture of any kind, no bed, no pad nor even blankets on the floor.

He settled to the floor with his back against a wall, facing the all-but-invisible door and wondered when it would open. He decided he was in some sort of a lock-up, probably a make-do confinement in a storage room inasmuch as Gold Stream wasn't yet big enough to afford a proper jailhouse. He leaned back against the wall and closed his eyes, trying to relieve the pounding pain in his head. From time to time, he opened them again to glance at the tiny window to see if dawn was on its way.

Dutch Snyder rolled over in his bed onto a sore spot at his ribs that brought him awake with a muttered oath. Easing onto his back, he stared at the dingy ceiling of his tiny room at the Gruber rooming house, the first slants of early morning sun beginning to brighten his bedchamber. He thought of the young man in the storage-room cell and considered rising to go to the jail and beat the hell out of him. He wondered if he'd be able to beat him to death—he'd never actually done it to anyone, but he'd come close a couple of times. Thinking about it, he rose up on one elbow and awakened a dozen different pains that young McKay had inflicted on him. He settled back into the bed for comfort and curled away from his aches and decided to delay revenge until he felt a little better. He considered the floral pattern wallpaper for a few more moments, then closed his eyes and tried to fall asleep again.

* * *

J. C. Farley was weary, his eyes burning for the lack
of sleep, his legs aching from the hours he'd stood
behind the bar of the Gold Strike Saloon. Two of the
men who'd come in with Jack Moss were still awake in
the barroom where they'd been steadily drinking,
seemingly not any more drunk now than they'd been at
midnight. Three others were asleep on the floor, one
snoring loudly. Moss and one other were upstairs,
either sleeping or taking turns with the girls. Joe
Calvecci had stayed on the floor with his bartender for
most of the evening, calm and composed, moving quietly and unobtrusively to ease his regular customers out
of the saloon before any confrontations might occur.
When only the desperadoes remained in the barroom,
Calvecci had worked with J. C. to serve them, giving no
arguments, practicing servility, showing no indication
of resentment or censure. Even so, it had been a rowdy
and unruly band of cutthroats describing in chilling
detail their assault upon Tom Patterson's ranch, celebrating the dreadful deaths by fire inflicted upon those
inside.

Calvecci and Farley had exchanged horrified
glances at the bragging accounts of the ranch burning
and realized that not only Patterson, but Betty and
young McKay had perished as well. Both saloon men
had masked their feelings, recognizing that their own
lives might depend upon maintaining an appearance of
disinterest.

At last, when the whiskey and the late hours brought
fatigue to the gang, Calvecci had retired to his own
rooms, promising to relieve J. C. soon after sunup.

J. C. looked at the clock on the wall and noted the

time to be close to eight o'clock. He gave a slight smile as he saw the proprietor at the top of the stairs, starting down, his steps heavy and without vitality. He looked like an old man as he descended the steps.

"You can get some sleep now, J. C. I'll take over."

"Got my second wind," the bartender told him. "I'll just keep you company."

Calvecci started to argue, then nodded appreciatively.

"Think it's true about Patterson and Betty?" J. C. asked in a low voice. "And the young fellow?"

Calvecci didn't answer for a few moments. "Too many witnesses not to be true. Terrible for all of them."

"Betty's fault for taking up with him," Farley said with a shake of his head. "Still, there ain't nothing bad I can ever think of that young lady. I'm going to miss her."

Calvecci's eyes misted slightly and, again, he nodded. "So will I, J. C. So will we all."

"I need some help," Tom said, twisting on the ladder to address Betty. "I ain't quite got the strength to lift this here trapdoor. There's something on the other side."

"Maybe it's still burning up there," Betty said, her voice coming out of the darkness. "Maybe we should wait."

"Naw, I think she's done," Tom countered. "Breathing seems easier. I 'spect the smoke ain't as thick and I don't hear so much of the fire as before." He bowed his head and pressed his bare shoulders to the trapdoor again. "Come on up on the ladder with me and

help me shove. Bring me something we can wedge in if
we can get her lifted."

There were sounds in the darkness as Betty rummaged through the cellar. Then, she was up on the ladder on the rung with him ready to try. "Found an old
piece of shelving that ought to do," she told him, then
took a deep breath. "I'm ready when you say."

"Now!" Tom said. He thrust his shoulders up and felt
the trapdoor move just a bit, then it rose a little more as
Betty joined in the effort. "By dern, she's coming!" he
shouted, a crack of daylight appearing. "Stick it in!"

Betty shoved the small board into the space.

"There!" Tom said. He reached out to make sure the
wedge was secure and then used it to lever up the trapdoor. He leaned close to the inch-high crack. "From
what I can see, fire's pretty well burned out. Some timbers still burning."

"What's holding us in?" Betty asked with concern.

"Maybe a rafter fell on it. Maybe something lighter."

"Can we get out?"

"We moved her a little. We ought to be able to push
our way out if we keep at it."

"What about them?"

"Long gone, I'd reckon," he said hopefully. "Come
on, Let's give 'er another try."

Together, they heaved up against the trapdoor and
were relieved to feel a sudden shifting of weight as
something slid off. With another shove, they swung the
door up and open.

Tom took a careful step up the ladder, his head
emerging from the cellar aperture. "Pretty toasty up

here," he commented. "Fire's still going pretty strong in some parts, but I think we can get out all right."

"What about Moss and his gang?" the young woman asked again.

"They're bound to be off somewhere," Tom said optimistically, not really able to see as much as he wanted. "Might as well find out for sure."

He pulled himself out of the opening, taking care to step around the smoldering timbers strewn about him. He looked around as he moved a few feet away and looked past the smoking ruin to the countryside beyond. After a few moments, he picked his way back to the cellar opening. "Come on," he told her, drawing a Colt out of a holster and cocking it. "Watch where you step and lift up your nightgown."

He waited until she joined him, his left hand reaching out for hers, holding the Colt at chest-level in his right. Together, they made their way through the smoking debris, avoiding the remnant timbers that were still burning intensely, careful to step over the searing coals from the cabin ruins that lay in their path.

Once out of the burning and blackened ruin, Tom scanned the landscape for any sign of the nightriders. Satisfied that they were alone, he returned the revolver to his holster. "Trouble with Jack Moss," he said, more to himself than to Betty, "never did have a lot of patience." Seeing the look on her face, he smiled and explained. "Should have made sure about us."

Betty's attention was suddenly focused on a dark mass on the ground near the still-smoldering debris of the barn. "What's that? Over there?"

"Nothing you want to go see," Tom answered. "Guess I got one of 'em."

"Moss?"

Tom shook his head. "Not likely."

"We just going to leave him there?"

"For the time being," Tom responded. "I sure as hell ain't going to take the time to bury him."

"That don't seem right."

"We got other things to worry about," Tom said.

"What will we do now?" she asked as she looked at her robe and nightgown, dirty and soot-smeared.

"Walk into Gold Stream, I reckon," he answered.

"Won't . . . they be there?" she asked, fear showing in her eyes and voice.

"Most likely," he said cheerfully. He reached to touch her under the chin, lifting her face to his, then embraced her. "But we don't need to fret about that too much. They think we're dead," he chuckled. "And we'll let 'em just keep thinking that till its time."

"Time?"

"For me to call out Jack Moss."

She pulled away from him to look into his eyes. "You ain't well enough, Tom! You're just getting over one gunfight and you're in no shape for another."

"Better it be me than young McKay."

"Matt?" she questioned, concern for both men dismaying her. "But he's gone home," she said.

"Someday, somewhere, Jack's going to find him and that'll be the end of Matt," he told her, then nodded to the ruins of his house. "Jack's made it my fight now."

Betty stood for a moment, then returned to the comfort of Tom's arms. "I just wish it could all go away."

Tom held her for a few moments more, then gently moved her back to arm's length. "It's a bit of a walk this morning, Bett, my darling," he said, nodding to the trail. "I guess we'd better get going."

Chapter Twenty

Dutch Snyder was annoyed as the miner, Bill, hurried into the restaurant tent and sat on the bench beside him, interrupting his breakfast. Snyder liked to be alone most of the time and didn't suffer intrusions lightly.

"Hear the news?" the pockmarked miner inquired, belatedly aware of Snyder's displeasure. "About the Moss gang?"

Snyder continued to fork fried mush into his mouth, his manner showing he was not all that interested.

"They're in town, right down there at the Gold Strike."

"Let Calvecci get his pet gunslinger to run 'em outta town," Snyder mumbled through his mouthful.

"That's what I'm telling ya!" the miner exulted. "He and his gang burned down the Patterson place last night with ol' Tom and that slut inside."

"Where'd you hear that?" Snyder asked, his breakfast now forgotten.

"It's all over town. They was in here late last night talking about it, bragging about it. They were after the McKay kid and thought they got him too."

"Anybody tell 'em different?"

"Not yet. Far as I know, Dutch, nobody saw us bring him in yesterday."

"What's their interest in him?" Snyder asked.

"Way I get it, young McKay done killed Jack Moss' younger brother. That's the reason he's been out there. His old man's been paying Patterson, teaching him to shoot."

"What for?" Snyder asked, not understanding.

"So he could stand up to Jack Moss," the miner said, his tone of voice betraying an impatience, which he instantly regretted.

Snyder gave the miner a hard shove, knocking him off the bench and onto the dirt floor. "Don't you give me any of that look, Bill, or I'll pound your head for you." He returned to his breakfast, ignoring the miner as he picked himself up and sat gingerly on the bench once again, his manner tentative and frightened.

"This may work out," Snyder said. "Been wondering myself what to do about McKay."

"Thought you were going to whack on him today," Bill said. "Gonna make him pay for yesterday."

"I'm thinking of something better," Snyder said gruffly. "Now, you get yourself down to the Gold Strike and let me know what's happening."

"Whatcha going to do, Dutch?"

"I'm still thinking about it," Snyder snarled. "Now, let me get on with my morning meal and go do what I told you."

The skinny miner rose with a nod of obedience and hurried out of the tent.

Snyder finished his bacon and mush, then sat for a few minutes, lingering over his bitter, black coffee. Finally, he rose, picked up his baton and walked out of the tent, passing the hopeful cashier, giving him neither a glance nor a dime. He walked out into the morning sunlight and moved toward the jail, making his plans. He passed Matt's still-saddled horse at the hitching rail, then unlocked and entered the two-room structure. Snyder cast a glance at the makeshift cell door, then moved to the chair behind a rough wooden table that served as a desk. There were no papers upon it, only Matt's gun belt, holster, and revolver. He laid his baton on the table, sat down with his hands behind his head and his feet on the table.

"Somebody out there?" came Matt's muffled voice.

Snyder disregarded the call.

"Snyder ? Open the door!"

"Shut up!" Snyder bellowed. "I'll tend to you when I get around to it!"

"You've got no cause to keep me here, Snyder!" Matt yelled. "You don't have any legal standing at all!"

"I got all I need, boy! You stop making a racket or I'll break your head!"

There was a series of thumps on the door, which Snyder ignored. He picked up Matt's double-action revolver, examined it, then smiled at a thought. He rose, stuck the revolver under his coat and walked out of the building.

He strode down the plank walk to the blacksmith's

shop and walked into the open shed. He raised a hand in a half-gesture of greeting to the man working at the forge. "Need a hammer, Smithy," he said gruffly, more as a demand than a request. The blacksmith gave him a shrug and pointed to a workbench. Snyder stepped to it, surveyed the assortment of tools, then selected a mallet and a chisel. With his back concealing his work from the busy blacksmith, he took out Matt's revolver and unloaded the chambers. He pulled back the hammer and placed the revolver into a bench-mounted vise and secured it. He placed the tip of the chisel against the firing tip of the hammer and brought the hammer down on the tool sharply, once, twice, and a third time, shearing the point from the mass of the hammer. He laid the tools aside and ran his thumb over the severed edge, then reached for a file. He ran the rasp back and forth over the rough edge, smoothing it. Releasing the revolver from the vise, he held it up for inspection. Satisfied, he reloaded the weapon, tucked it back under his coat and walked out of the shed with a curt nod to the disinterested blacksmith.

He moved behind the string of buildings on his return, stopping behind one, out of sight. He took out the revolver and pointed it to the ground, then pulled the trigger. There was the sound of a snap, but no explosion. Pleased with his handiwork, he snapped the hammer several times, making sure that it would misfire each time. More than satisfied, he returned to the jail where he returned the revolver to Matt's holster.

"Snyder?" Matt shouted. "Open this door!"

"Keep your shirt on!" Snyder yelled in high, good

humor. "I might just do that after awhile!" He started to reach for the baton, thought better of it, then walked out of the building.

At the Gold Strike, he saw Bill and several others standing at the entrance, all trying to see what was going on inside.

Bill caught sight of Snyder. "They're still in there, but they're fixing to leave pretty soon now." Then, he added, "I done saw Jack Moss hisself standing there at the bar."

"How soon they leaving?" Snyder asked.

"Don't rightly know," Bill replied with shake of his head. "Heard some of 'em say they ain't feeling well enough to ride."

Snyder studied the door of the saloon for a few moments, then fished in his pocket for a key. "Here," he said and handed it to Bill, "you take this over to the jail and let that McKay out in, say, fifteen minutes."

"Let him out?"

"That's right," Snyder instructed. "Let him out and be sure to give him back his gun."

"Where are you going?" Bill asked.

"In there," Snyder said, pointing to the saloon. "I think Mr. Moss just might be interested in finding out that young McKay didn't get burned up in that fire."

A slow smile of comprehension came over Bill's face. "I'll bet he would at that, Dutch."

"Fifteen minutes," Snyder repeated. "And you make sure he gets his gun, you hear?"

"I'm going, Dutch. On my way."

Snyder watched the miner as he hurried in the direction of the jail, then turned and walked toward the saloon. The gathering of men parted as he approached, most of them showing surprise at his arrival.

"You going in there, Dutch?" one asked sarcastically. "Thought you'd be long gone outta town by now."

"Maybe he don't know Jack Moss is in there," said another.

Snyder growled an unintelligible retort and pushed through the doors into the saloon. It took a few seconds for his eyes to adjust from the bright sunlight to the comparative gloom of the barroom. Four men lounged at one table, two at another. Behind the bar, Farley and Calvecci were watching a sinister, bearded man at the counter as he poured a drink from a bottle.

All conversation stopped and all eyes turned to the intruder.

"I'd like a word with Mr. Moss," Snyder said with awkward servility.

No one responded.

"It's about something he ought to know," Snyder added, almost as a whine.

"What is it, fat ass?" the bearded man said.

Snyder was flabbergasted at the insult and wondered if he hadn't made a dreadful mistake. He cast a worried look at Calvecci. "Well, sir, it's something kinda private and—"

"Say your piece or get outta here," Moss cut in.

"It's about the McKay kid," Snyder managed to say. "Something you don't know."

He was aware of the sharp looks of the two men behind the bar.

"Ain't nothing I need to know," the outlaw said. "He's been fried along with ol' Tom."

"Begging your pardon, Mr. Moss," Snyder persisted. "Young McKay warn't out at the Patterson place last night."

Moss turned his full attention to the heavyset man while, behind him, Calvecci and J.C. glanced at one another, then glared at Snyder.

"He's . . . well, he's up at the jail," Snyder said, stumbling over his words. "We . . . ah . . . picked him up going past town yesterday evening and locked him up."

"Goddamn it, Snyder," J.C. began in outrage. "You ain't got a decent bone—"

"Shut up," Moss cut in, taking a few steps forward. "You some sort of a lawman, are you?"

Snyder was suddenly conscious of his badge under his coat. "Well, not really, Mr. Moss," he said hurriedly. He whisked the badge from his shirt and into his pocket. "I just help out when the miners get a little rowdy. I ain't really no official kinda lawman at all." He paused, worried. "You can ask Mr. Calvecci there. He'll tell you that I ain't any kind of a lawdog."

Calvecci gave no answer, a look of cold loathing on his face.

"If you was a mind to do something about that McKay fella," Snyder offered, "he'll be on the street any minute now."

"Do what, fatso?" Moss asked.

"Well, he's been trying to learn how to shoot if you was to call him out," Snyder explained. "I figger he ain't no match for you."

"Maybe Patterson taught him better'n you think," Moss countered.

"It won't be no contest at all . . . not with that gun he's carrying," Snyder said with a sly wink. "I made sure of that."

"You saying something's wrong with his gun?" Moss asked.

Snyder nodded and gave a slight smile. "Yessir. He's gonna get a great big surprise when he goes to shoot it."

"What's your part in this, fat man?" Moss asked as he stepped close to Snyder, his eyes searching. "Young McKay put them marks on you?"

Discomfited, Snyder took a step backward, not able to make a reply.

"Get your fat butt outta here," Moss said with contempt, then added with sarcasm, "but I do thank you for your information."

Snyder stood for a long few seconds, stunned by the humiliation and frightened by the wintry look on the outlaw's face. "Just trying to do you a turn," he muttered as he walked toward the door.

"You're done in Gold Stream, Snyder," Calvecci called after him. "As of this day."

"Wouldn't count on that, Calvecci, but it sure is over and done for that McKay," Snyder shot back as he strode from the saloon.

"We ought to do something," J. C. whispered to his boss.

Calvecci gave a grimace. "What in the name of heaven can we do?"

Chapter Twenty-one

As the bedraggled pair reached the west side of Gold Stream, Tom stopped and warily scanned the mining settlement.

"Don't stop, Tom," Betty groaned, looking down in dismay at her torn, ruined robe and nightgown, then at her wrecked, soft-soled slippers. "If I stop now, I don't know that I can get going again."

"They ain't the best shoes for walking, are they?" Tom commented with a quick glance at her slippers. He pointed toward the Gold Strike. "Bunch of horses there at the Gold Strike."

"There always are," Betty said, weary and impatient.

"Most likely Jack Moss and his bunch," Tom said, more to himself than to Betty. "Best we move around the town's backsides to get to Nate's place." Tom stepped out at a brisk pace. "Let's keep going."

"What are you going to do if he's here in town?" she asked as she hurried alongside him.

"Kill him if I can."

"All by yourself?" Betty scoffed. "All his men?"

"Jack's the one I'll worry about first," Tom said. "We'll see about the others when it's time."

"Isn't there some kind of law somewhere, Tom?" she argued. "You and me can swear that they tried to kill us."

"Well, there's territorial law down there in Denver," Tom replied as he veered off the main road, leading Betty around the laundry tent. Inside, several Chinese men looked up from their steaming tubs to stare as the tattered pair walked past.

"We must look a fright," Betty said, ashamed to be seen. She resumed her entreaty, "Couldn't we just go on to Denver? Go there and do what they call it . . . testify? Tell 'em about Moss and what he's done?"

"Ain't got much faith in what they'd do, Bett," he answered. "Someday, they might do something, maybe, but that don't solve much right now."

They trudged on, moving past the tents, thankful that the breakfast hour was long past in the restaurant tents and too early for the gambling saloons to have many customers.

Even so, Tom and Betty's passage aroused the curiosity of two late diners who rose from their table and stepped to the open flaps of the canvas-covered eatery establishment to confirm what they'd glimpsed.

"Ain't that Tom Patterson?" one asked incredulously, a tall middle-aged man in a rancher's hat. "And Miss Betty, too."

"He ain't wearing a shirt," his short, stout companion responded.

"Looks like they ain't dead after all."

"I wonder if Jack Moss knows about that?" the short man said.

"I sure ain't going to be the one who tells him," volunteered his companion. "Reckon they'll all work that out for themselves."

"Be interesting to watch," the short man ventured. "Let's go finish our breakfast and then see what happens."

Tom and Betty reached the back door of the Gold Stream Mercantile and Tom banged on it impatiently.

After a few moments, Nate opened it and filled the frame. "My Lord!" he exclaimed. "Word is that you're dead!" He shifted his gaze to Betty. "Both of you."

"If you wouldn't mind, Mr. Wainscote," Betty said. "Can we talk about it inside?" She looked at him imploringly. "Do you have something for me to put on?"

"Come in, come in," the big man said in apology. "Sure, we'll find something for you." He looked at their grimy faces. "You can use my tub," he offered as he stepped aside for the pair to enter. He nodded to a stairway that led to an upper floor. "I'll bring the hot water."

"Ain't got time for that myself," Tom said. "Is Jack Moss in town?"

Nate nodded. "He and his bunch have been down at the Gold Strike all night. They've been bragging as to how they killed everybody at your place." He paused. "What really happened?"

"Came in the middle of the night," Tom answered as he pulled one of his Colts to check it. "Burned the barn with the horses inside, then fired the house. Thought they burned us with it. As you can see, they didn't get the job done."

"What happened to the young fellow?"

"Rode out yesterday before they came," Tom told him. He started walking through the store, Nate following. Betty, despite her fatigue, was unable to restrain her curiosity and walked after them.

"I'll help myself to a shirt if you don't mind," Tom said, only half-asking. He took a flannel shirt from a shelf, put it on, buttoned it and tucked the tail into his jeans. "Anybody know what they're doing right now?"

"Been drinking and whoring all night," Nate said, casting a self-conscious look at Betty. "They're probably not in too good a shape after a wild night."

"Well, maybe that'll help some, make us even," Tom said with bleak humor. "I've been freezing and roasting all night in a danged cellar." He laughed. "My fingers are so froze up, I'll probably drop my dern pistol."

"You going against them?" Nate asked. "All of them?"

Tom nodded. "Jack, alone, if he'll come out."

"And what if he won't?" Betty asked in vexation.

Tom shrugged. "Hope somebody will help, I reckon."

Nate nodded in return. "I'll back you, Tom."

"I'd appreciate it, Nate."

"If you'd give me just a few minutes," the giant store-keeper said, "I think I can get some others to help."

A look of impatience crossed Tom's face.

"He's right, Tom," Betty said, a tone of appeal in her voice. "It's not just you and Nate against him, it's all of them."

Tom started to argue, then gave both of them a smile of agreement. "Come to think of it, I wasn't all that handy the last time out, was I?" Then, he turned serious. "Get to it, Nate. I wouldn't want 'em to get outta town before I'm finished with 'em."

"Back in five minutes," Nate said, hurrying away.

Matt was dozing when the door opened and the pockmarked miner stood in the doorway. "Dutch said you can leave."

"Nice of him," Matt muttered as he rose to his feet and walked into the outer room.

"Get your gun there," the miner said, pointing to weapon on the desk. "Dutch said to make sure you got it."

Matt picked up the gun belt and strapped it around his waist. "What's his concern about it? Am I going to need it?"

"Jack Moss is in town."

Matt turned, showing his surprise. "Where?"

"At the Gold Strike. Rode in after killing Tom Patterson," the man said, enjoying telling the news, delighted at the look of anguish on the young man's face.

"Tom? What about Betty?"

"The whore?" The man laughed. "She got cooked right along with ol' Tom."

"Cooked?" Matt exclaimed, dread overwhelming him. "What do you mean?"

Again, the miner cackled. "Well, Jack and his bunch fired the house and burned it down. Thought you was in there too." He smiled, showing his ugly teeth. "I'd light out of town before he finds out about you."

"Thanks," Matt said. He considered the baton on the table. Instead, he swung his fist against the man's chin, dropping him senseless to the floor. "Appreciate your concern."

He walked out of the building to the hitching rail where his horse snorted at the sight of him. He gave the animal a comforting pat, then glanced down at the Colt Lightning in his holster. Thinking of the miner's odd insistence about taking his gun, he pulled the revolver and examined it. He opened the cylinder and checked the load. He started to return it to his holster, then noticed a tiny speck of metal caught between the frame and the walnut stock. He pulled back the hammer and immediately saw the damage to the firing pin. He pointed the revolver at the ground and pulled the trigger. He smiled bitterly at the snapping sound.

He opened a saddlebag, unfastened his gun belt and exchanged it and the damaged weapon for the belt with the old Walker. He checked the load, holstered the heavy revolver and reached into the pouch for a second cylinder. He put the spare in his pocket and turned his gaze toward the Gold Strike.

Do I do this? Can I do this?

He gave his horse another pat, then started toward the saloon, his stride slow and tentative at first, then lengthening with determination.

Chapter Twenty-two

"**I** got a couple of volunteers, Tom," Nate said as he entered the store with two young men behind him. "You know Beck and Zimmerman."

Tom recognized both as reputable, hard-working miners. "Thanks, John," Tom said, extending his hand to the first, a small wiry man with a head of red hair.

"We'll do what we can," Beck responded, shaking hands.

"I ain't much on handguns, but I can handle a rifle pretty good," the second man, Zimmerman, said. The larger man, undersized compared to Nate, held up a rifle to show that he was prepared.

"And thanks to you . . . it's Ben?"

"Bud," the man corrected. "Bud Zimmerman."

"Thanks, Bud." Tom looked at the group facing him. "You know what you're getting into so I won't waste time over it. If Jack gets me, it's best that you all just let 'em ride on outta town. If I get him and his men come

190

out, you people give a few shots from cover to let 'em know there's more than one—"

"Tom!" Betty shouted with sudden alarm.

All turned to her, seeing her flustered and dismayed by the door, her eyes on the street outside. "It's Matt!"

At once, Tom came to her side. "What the hell is he doing here?"

Matt was about thirty feet past their building, walking toward the Gold Strike. Down the street at the saloon building, Jack Moss stepped out of the shadows into the sunlight and stopped, waiting. Behind him, members of his gang had come out to watch.

"Matt!" Tom yelled as he rushed out the door.

Matt stopped in surprise and turned, a wide smile growing on his lips. "You all right, Tom?"

"I'm fine, Matt," Tom called, "Betty, too. She's in the store with Nate." He hurried after Matt and came within ten feet. "Back off from him, Matt. It's my fight now."

Matt hesitated, the proposition was appealing. Then, he shook his head. "You'll have to wait your turn, Tom. This all started with me and I've got to finish it."

"Tom?" Moss shouted from the distance. "How the hell did you stay alive?"

"'Cause I ain't as dumb as you, Jack! If you'd had a lick of sense, you'd have made sure about us before you rode off to do your celebrating!"

"Well, I'll make damned sure of it now!"

"I can handle him," Matt said, intervening before Tom could reply. "You taught me."

"I didn't teach you that good, boy," Tom said in exasperation. "He's a killer and you ain't. He knows how and you don't."

"I've killed before remember . . . his brother."

"That was a damned fluke and you know it! You ain't the killing kind."

"Stay outta this, Tom!" shouted Moss. "This here's between me and my kid brother's killer!"

"You already murdered his pa! Ain't that enough killing fer you?" Tom yelled.

"You mix in and we'll kill every living soul in this here saloon . . . and any others we feel like!"

"Damned if he wouldn't," Tom said to himself.

"Fair fight, Tom!" the outlaw declared. "Just between me and him! I take care of him, my boys ride on outta town with no other shooting! Even if it's the other way round and he gets me, Bob and the boys leave and nobody else gets hurt!"

"Why do I doubt your word, Jack?"

"Tom, this is my problem," Matt interjected. "Like you said, he killed my pa . . . and it's something *I've* got to do. Don't you see?"

"No, son, I really don't," Tom argued. "You're fixing to get yourself killed."

"He'll do it, Tom. Unless I face him, he'll kill Joe, J. C., and the girls. You know that."

Tom glanced at Moss and sized up the situation. With reluctance, he nodded. "Moss!" he shouted. "You make it a fair fight, you hear?"

"Fair fight it'll be!" Moss answered.

"You and me, we still got a score to settle!" Tom exclaimed.

"That'll hafta wait for a different day 'less you want your saloon folks with holes in 'em!"

Tom turned to Matt. "Don't let him get close. You

got that Walker. Pull 'er now and don't try to draw with him. Ain't nobody's going to blame you or make anything like a goddamn thing of honor out of it."

Matt didn't argue, but the Walker remained holstered.

"Well, it's your funeral," Tom said in disgust.

"Thanks for that thought," Matt responded.

With a sigh, Tom made a yielding gesture to Moss and walked back to stand by the porch of the mercantile building.

The town was as quiet as a church in silent prayer. An occasional fitful breeze gave a keening sound as it gusted through the buildings and momentarily swirled old newspaper pages, crumpled notices and other debris from the street. Matt's eyes swept the storefronts, knowing that there were people inside those buildings, peering out, willing to risk errant gunfire rather than to miss the show.

Eager to see me die. God, I'm scared.

Moss started walking forward, still a considerable distance away. He walked to his right, angling toward the other side of the street, his movements steady and deliberate. There was a manner about him that spoke of past experience, of confidence and disdain for this opponent as it had been for others.

Matt remained where he stood, his eyes following Moss with his right hand hovering over the Walker.

"How good is he, Tom?" Moss shouted. "Can he shoot them cans and bottles? He ever face a real gun?"

Matt remembered how the gunman, Deiter, had kept up a steady stream of talk when he started shooting. Matt stepped into his forty-five degree stance and waited.

"How did ya have him practicing fast draw?" Moss continued, moving closer. "Oh, I know he's handy with a shotgun against a liquored-up youngster, but I think he's scared to death of me!"

Trying to get closer. Talking to make me nervous, to get within his range.

"Stand right where you are, Moss!" Matt shouted.

Moss ignored him and kept coming. "I'll do what I damn well please you young—"

Instinct galvanized Matt and he suddenly dashed right.

Moss was still talking and walking when he drew and fired, the boom of his revolver blasting over his words.

Matt heard the bullet buzz past his left ear as he drew the heavy weapon and promptly fumbled it to the ground. Desperately, he bent down to scramble after it and his clumsiness saved him as bullets sped over his head. He stood erect and slapped the Walker into his left hand, taking his stance in his peculiar shooting posture. He fired two shots hurriedly, knowing they were wild.

Moss came to a standstill, a look of surprise and consternation on his face. For a moment, he looked away, uncertainty in his manner.

Matt fired again and missed.

Another bullet then sang past Matt's face.

Matt took his time as he ran to his right. He made a sharp move to his left, then a dodge back to the right and aimed the Walker.

Before he could fire, Moss's next shot caught Matt

high on the left shoulder. The Walker sagged in his hands as a scalding pain cut across him, as though a sword had been drawn across the skin.

With a cry of triumph, Moss stopped full, aiming for the killing shot. His revolver clicked on empty. He reached for another gun in a second holster.

Matt ignored the stinging pain and stepped into his stance again. He brought the heavy weapon up into his two-handed hold, aimed carefully and pulled the trigger.

The first shot missed just as Moss brought up his loaded weapon. Two bullets cut the air ever so near their target, but Matt steadied his aim.

Hit the post! Just like hitting the post!

Matt squeezed the trigger gently and his next shot hit Moss in the chest and slammed him to the ground. Matt took a few steps forward and, again, aimed carefully. This bullet caught the outlaw in the head and blasted his life away.

The Walker clicked on an empty chamber and Matt lowered it almost in disbelief, astonished to see the desperado sprawled on the dusty street. Beyond him, members of the Moss gang were rushing forward, astounded and angered at the death of their leader.

Their fury centered on the still standing survivor.

Hurriedly, Matt snapped out the spent cylinder and reached for the spare in his pocket. As he pulled it out, it slipped from his fingers and tumbled to the ground, bouncing away behind him.

Bob Daly took a few steps forward and stared hard at his fallen leader. With his own six-gun drawn, he turned his attention to Matt, his gaze traveling from the empty gun to the out-of-reach cylinder. He raised his revolver and snapped off a shot at Matt, the bullet buzzing across the ground three feet away from him.

Instantly, there was return fire from Tom's revolver as he sprinted to Matt's side, covering him as they scurried in retreat. Matt reached down to retrieve the spare cylinder as they rushed past.

"So much fer Jack's promises," Tom said as they reached cover behind a water trough. "How bad you hit?"

"Just grazed, I think," Matt replied, lifting his shirt to peer at his shoulder. "Hurts like hell, but I don't think it's too deep." Nonetheless, a sudden sheen of perspiration appeared on his face as he sought to retain his senses. "Got to reload," he muttered as he snapped in the second cylinder.

"Your work's over for the day, boy," Tom told him.

The young man shook his head in disagreement, then nodded to indicate the threat of the advancing outlaws. "Now's no time to talk about it."

A bullet thumped into the wooden trough.

"Danged if this isn't the same damned trough I was behind in my last shooting match," Tom said in some wonderment.

"It was the one in front of the store," Matt told him with a grin. He hefted the Walker again, ready to fire.

"Tom!" came Betty's voice, loud and anxious. "Is Matt bad off?"

"Naw!" Tom bellowed. "Just a little chunk of meat gone. Gonna be just fine!" A bullet whined down the street and attracted his attention. "Gotta get to work, Bett!" He raised his head to see over the water trough and ducked quickly as another shot hit close. "They're making a fight of it, boys!" he yelled. "John! You and Bud come with me! Nate, come take care of Matt!"

The two miners, Zimmerman and Beck came out of the general store, crouching low with rifles in their hands. Tom waved them across the street and Nate, with his rifle held high, lumbered to join Matt and Tom. The big man hunkered down beside Matt, his bulk inadequately shielded by the water trough.

"It'd be real smart of you to stay right here," Tom advised Matt, then dashed across the street to join the two miners.

The Moss gang faltered at the arrival of support. First two of them, then another two started backing away, leaving only Daly and one other outlaw still firing in the middle of the street.

Peering around the corner of a building, Tom cupped his hands to shout down the center of the town. "Anybody wants a part of the fun, come on! We're going to run what's left of the Moss bunch outta town!"

Despite Nate's protest, Matt pushed up from behind the trough and made a run for a wagon close to the Gold Strike, bullets stitching into the ground at his feet. Reaching cover, he fired a shot at the men retreating into the saloon.

"Danged fool kid," Tom muttered with some admiration. He glanced around to see a couple of new townsmen, stooping low, coming out of buildings behind him to join the fight. "I thank you for your help!" he shouted. "Please don't get yourself killed if you can help it!"

He fired twice, then rose from concealment and made another dash, finding cover behind a building across the street from the Gold Strike. A moment later, Beck and Zimmerman sprinted into the space beside him, a hail of bullets arriving too late to injure them. Down the street he saw Nate and another townsman edging toward the saloon, hiding themselves behind stacked crates outside the freight office. The two outlaws in the street were now in retreat. Daly fired his last shot and dashed toward the Gold Strike with his henchman close behind.

"They're on the run, boys!" Tom shouted. "Let 'em have it!"

As if on command, a volley of shots thundered from both sides of the street into the saloon.

"Tom!" came a worried voice from inside. "You're going to wreck my place!"

"Sorry, Joe!" Tom shouted back. "We know how you prize your property!" He held up his hand to signal a halt to the firing. "Tell them fellas in there that if they've got a mind to live, we'll hold up long enough for them to get to their horses and get outta town!"

There was a long silence, then a barrage of gunfire came from the saloon, driving every man on the street to cover.

"Well, Joe, we gave 'em a chance! Sorry about the damage!" He took careful aim at what appeared to be a silhouette through a window. He fired, the shot shattering the glass and a figure staggered away, then fell.

"You all right, Joe?" Tom yelled.

There was no answer.

"How about J. C.? And the girls?"

An upstairs window shot up and Wanda stuck her head out. "We're all right, Tom! J. C.'s up here with us! I think Mr. Joe's all right too! He's down under the bar!"

"Duck back in there, Wanda!" Tom shouted. "You don't want to catch any stray bullets up there!"

Instantly, the window closed.

"What's the next move, Tom?" Nate called.

"Some of you work your way around to the back, in case anybody's going out that way!"

"We'll shoot this old Eye-talian in here, Patterson!" Daly's voice declared. "'Less you clear out and let us outta here!"

"Hell's bells!" Tom shouted in exasperation. "We made that offer to you just a minute ago!" He paused to consider. "Naw, I don't think so! You had your chance! Now, we're going to put all of you in jail!"

"What about the Eye-talian?" came the incredulous question from Daly.

"Well, if you kill Joe, I guess we'll hafta hang the bunch of ya!

"All of us?" asked another voice, strained with anxiety.

"We ain't got any judge here in Gold Stream!" Tom proclaimed with righteous gravity. "Ain't no way for us to tell who's worse than the other! 'Sides, all you being hung at the same time would be mighty entertaining for folks!"

There was a long period of silence.

"We could hurt those girls upstairs!" Daly's voice threatened. "The Eye-talian and the barkeep too!"

"That'd be pretty nasty of you," Tom called back,

"seeing as how they've done their best all night to give you a good time!" He paused, then added, "And it'd be your last good time! We'd have to make those hangings slow and over a roasting fire!"

Again, there was a long silence.

Then came a short intense argument, the words unclear, but spoken with temper.

Then, a gunshot.

"Can we take you up on riding outta here?" a new voice pleaded loudly. "Bob, here, wouldn't let the rest of us have a say the first time!"

"Well, what's he got to say about it now?"

"Bob ain't going to be saying anything anymore!" the new voice informed them. "We'd like to make a new deal!"

Tom glanced at the men behind him, then across to the small group on the other side. He made a decision. "All right!" he called. "You men! Hold your fire!" He raised a restraining hand, then addressed the outlaws, "In the Gold Strike—leave your firearms inside and come out the front door with your hands in the air!"

"You'll shoot us if we ain't got guns!"

"We'll shoot you fer sure if ya got 'em!"

A few moments later, the first man came through the door, hands high, moving with caution and fear. "We're gonna need our guns someplace else!" the outlaw complained, his voice identifying him as the new gang spokesman.

"Maybe you can steal some new ones!" Tom told him. "Or maybe some other owlhoots will shoot you and steal your horses! We don't care! Good riddance!"

The remaining members of the gang came inching

out into the sunlight, hands turned up, empty holsters on their hips.

"Get on your horses and get outta town!" Tom instructed as he moved out of the cover of the building. "Joe!" he called. "Anybody else in there?"

"All out except a couple of dead men, Tom!" came the reply, a note of resentment entering the proprietor's voice. "Were you really going to let them shoot me?"

Tom didn't answer immediately. "Well, we'd have done what we had to do, Joe!" he shouted finally, letting that stand as his answer.

Tom and the others formed a ring around the group of four subdued outlaws.

"Are we just going to let them ride out?" the miner, Beck, wanted to know.

"Gave 'em my word," Tom replied promptly. He waved his Colt at the desperados. "Get outta here before I change my mind."

The outlaws hurried to the hitching rails to untie their horses.

"The rifles too!" Tom instructed. "Dump 'em!"

Under the guns of the now considerable crowd, the cringing bandits carefully pulled their rifles from saddle holsters and laid them on the ground. With a collective look of askance, they mounted their horses in desperate haste.

"It's a shame," Matt said in a tone of reproach, moving over to stand beside Tom. "We let them go, they'll just go onto do bad things and kill other people."

The desperados spurred their horses and galloped down the main street, heading east out of town. Before the dust settled, men and women came streaming out of the tents and buildings, hurrying toward the Gold Strike. Betty, with a man's coat over her nightgown, ran barefooted to hug both Tom and Matt.

Matt suddenly sagged, giving in, more to relief than to the pain he'd repressed during the gunfight. Tom caught his good arm and steadied him, taking the heavy Walker that he handed to Nate.

"How'd I do?" Matt asked.

For a moment, those surrounding him did not understand.

Betty was the first. "You were wonderful," she said. "You were so brave."

Then, suddenly, there was a single chuckle and then a chortle began to ripple through the crowd.

"Lordy, son," came one comment. "You were just plain lucky."

"Bet ol' Jack Moss needed glasses," another declared, snickering over his observation. "You look in his pockets, I'll bet you'd find a pair of specs that he should've been wearing."

"You got sand, kid, I'll give you that," Beck said. "But sure as blazes, you ain't no gunfighter."

"Shoots like a girl! Using both hands!" offered a different voice. "Never saw anything like it!"

"Leave him be!" shouted a burly townsman. "Ain't none of you had what it takes to face Jack Moss and his gang, no matter how funny it looked!"

For a moment, Matt was crestfallen, somewhat hurt by the comments as he looked to Tom for confirmation.

A wide grin came to Tom's face, a smile he'd tried to contain. Then, the smile gave way to helpless laughter. "Lordy, Matt," he sputtered between spasms of mirth, "you're the clumsiest gunfighter I ever did see." He reeled away, holding his sides as he cackled, emitting great whoops of laughter.

Throughout the crowd, everyone was laughing with the exception of Matt and Betty, the latter mad at them all, but specifically at Tom.

Then, Matt began to snigger as well, a deep chuckle welling up from within, breaking into convulsions of laughter.

Betty was furious, standing with her hands on her hips, glaring at the howling, guffawing crowd, sending darts of enraged scowls at Tom, Nate, Beck and Zimmerman. "I just plain don't understand you people!" she declared fiercely. "Don't you dare laugh at him!" She turned, just as angry at Matt. "You march yourself into the Gold Strike! You need doctoring and, by God, you're going to get it!"

Matt's laughter ebbed at the force of her words, the pain in his shoulder intensifying, making him lightheaded once again. He nodded dutifully and started toward the saloon, his legs suddenly weak, his gait unsteady.

Around him, the laughter subsided into merriment as the crowd watched him anxiously.

"You there!" Betty said pointing to Bud Zimmerman. "Get him inside and help him up the stairs!" She raised her voice to shout for assistance. "Wanda!"

The upstairs window opened again and the saloon girl poked her head out.

"Put him in my bed while I go get the Chinaman!" Betty instructed.

"Hell, no!" Wanda shouted back. "I want him in my bed!"

"Not before we buy him a drink!" exclaimed a townsman. "No matter how he did it, the town owes him!"

A roar of approval came from the crowd as they surged toward the saloon, their chuckles blending into a joyous celebration.

"Now hold on!" Tom said with sharp authority. "There'll be time for that later on!"

The crowd stopped and turned to him, puzzled at his tone of command.

"I'm forming a posse," he declared. "Going after the Moss gang."

John Beck was the first to question. "Didn't you just tell 'em that they could leave? Gave 'em your word?"

"I told 'em they could leave," Tom explained. "Never said we wouldn't go after 'em."

"You, ah, got the authority to form a posse, Tom?" an older man asked. "Not that I'm saying you don't."

"Well, we could take a vote on it, I guess," Tom said soberly. "All in favor of going after 'em, raise your hands."

Not one hand came up.

"They ain't got any guns," Tom reminded them.

A dozen hands went up.

"They'll likely be just a couple of miles outta town," Tom said in speculation. "Likely they're all talking together, trying how to figure out how to come back here someday to get even."

A dozen more hands shot up.

"Okay," Tom told them. "Get saddled up and ready to go in ten minutes. "It's time to bring some law and order to Gold Stream!"

Chapter Twenty-three

A week later, at mid-morning, Matt gathered his few belongings and said his good-byes to the girls who were just rising after a long night's work. He came down the steps into the saloon and gave a tip of his hat to J. C. behind the bar.

"Ready to travel, are you?" Joe Calvecci turned away from supervising the workmen repairing bullet holes in the walls. They were carefully filling in the holes with patching plaster while a second crew was repainting. The shattered windows remained boarded, new glass on order out of Denver. Calvecci glanced at Matt's shoulder and nodded to it. "Healed up enough to ride?"

"Oh, yeah, only nicked me and it's fine. It's time to get home, Mr. Calvecci," he said with a nod, looking around. "Seen Betty?"

"She was up early," the proprietor told him. "She's out with her buggy somewhere. Did she know you were leaving?"

Matt shook his head. "Didn't know for sure myself till this morning. Thought I might as well." He paused, then added, "I wouldn't want to leave without saying good-bye."

"It'd hurt her if you did," Calvecci said, reaching out to shake Matt's hand. "You ought to sell out and settle here, Matt. Gold Stream's going to be a big town one of these days."

"Don't doubt it a bit, but we've . . . I've got a good business in Nebraska City. That is, it will be if I get back to it. Got a letter telling me that it's been closed since Pa died."

Calvecci nodded and walked to the front door of his establishment and looked out. "I think that's her buggy coming now," he said, peering across the tops of the café doors. "Tom's with her."

Matt smiled. "That's good. I've not seen much of Tom lately."

He and Calvecci moved through the louvered doors and onto the boardwalk.

Betty drove her buggy up to the front of the Gold Strike and waited until Tom stepped off and hurried around to help her down. "I knew it," Betty exclaimed, looking at Matt, glancing at the saddle pack in his hands and his horse at the hitching rail. "I knew this would be the day Matt would be leaving us."

"Where you've been, Tom?" Matt asked. "Your house is gone. I thought you'd be staying someplace here in town."

"I've been staying at that busted down place up there across the meadow," Tom replied. "It ain't near as bad as I thought it might be. The roof's got a couple of holes in it, but it'll do through what's left of the summer and a little bit into the fall."

"Why not stay in town?" Matt asked.

"I tried it for a few days. Stayed there in the jail with a bedroll," Tom explained. "Kinda hoped that Dutch Snyder might come sneaking back to town, but I guess not. Feller told me he's lit out for good." He shook his head and waved his hand to indicate the entire town. "Danged pests here always badgering me," he grumbled. "Some jasper or the another wanting to buy me a drink and ask me fool questions about the gunfight."

"Me too," Matt agreed with a grin. "Although I didn't think you'd object to a drink or two."

"It ain't the drinks . . . it's the company."

"Tom's giving up drinking," Betty interjected. "Made me a promise."

Tom gave her a look, then slowly nodded.

"You going to keep staying out there?" Matt asked.

"Yeah," Tom answered. "Be a place to sleep till I get the house and barn rebuilt. With the money your pa gave me, I ought to be able to get a good start at it."

"You've got more coming," Matt reminded him.

"I've got plenty as it is," Tom said firmly, waving off the subject. "Don't figger I did much of a job."

"It's Jack Moss in the graveyard, not me," Matt responded with a big grin. "I think that satisfies the terms of the agreement."

"Well . . ." Tom looked at Betty as if for permission, "we might find it helpful."

"We?"

Tom nodded, self-conscious in his manner. "Yeah,

208   *Jerry S. Drake*

we figgered that we'd been through a lot together so we might as well make 'er for the long haul."

Betty nodded happily, giving Tom's arm a squeeze.

"So you're going home?" Tom asked, uncomfortable at Betty's show of affection.

Matt nodded and tilted his head to the saloon owner. "Like I told Mr. Calvecci, it's time to get back and get my life going again."

"Going to be an old bachelor storekeep in Nebraska City?" Betty teased.

Matt laughed and shook his head. "Well, I've been away a spell. I think I told you that there was a certain young lady who I've kept in mind. Maybe she's kept thinking of me as well. You'll sure get an invitation to the wedding . . . if and when there ever is one."

He turned to Tom and grasped his hand. "Thanks, Tom," he said in earnest gratitude. "It may have been more luck than skill, but I think you're the reason I made it."

Tom gave an embarrassed shrug. "Well, maybe so, but . . . Lordy, Matt, don't ever tell a soul you learned your gun fighting from me."

With a hug from Betty and more handshakes with Tom and Calvecci, Matt untied the reins and swung up on his horse. With a wave good-bye, he spurred the roan away and trotted down the dusty street, heading east.

"Such a nice boy," Betty said, a catch in her voice. "I'll miss him." She turned to Tom, a troubled look on her face. "If, someday, we'd go to Nebraska City . . . like to a wedding, I mean," she said haltingly, "you don't suppose we'd embarrass him?"

Tom made a face and gave a dismissive gesture with his hand. "Lordy, Betty, we can be . . ." He stopped, searching for the word, "respectable if we'd want to be."

"You quitting me, Miss Betty?" Calvecci asked, suddenly anxious. "If I understand what you're saying. . . ."

"Oh, there ain't no rush about it, Joe," Betty said reassuringly. "I'll stay on till we get the house built. 'Course, there ain't going to be any more upstairs work, you understand?"

"You going to make it legal and all?" Calvecci asked, his gaze shifting back and forth between Betty and Tom. "Even a preacher?"

"You bet we are!" Tom declared.

"Well, I'll be damned," Calvecci exclaimed, then turned and walked through the swinging doors into his saloon.

Tom waited until he was sure that Calvecci was out of earshot. "Miss Betty," he said in a low, most respectful voice, his feet moving restlessly, nervously on the boardwalk, "now that we've decided . . ." he hesitated, clearing his throat, "it's embarrassing . . . I've always been meaning to ask."

Betty stood very still, trying not to show her exasperation. "Meaning to ask what, Tom?"

Tom took a moment more, studying the toes of his boots, a flush coming to his face. "Darling, I've always been meaning to ask . . . just what *is* your last name?"

Epilogue

Nathan Wainscote examined the envelope carefully and deliberated for several minutes. Finally, he reached for a letter opener and slid it under the flap. Inside, a folded letter enclosed a smaller envelope that he also opened. He read the wedding invitation with a slight smile and nodded his approval. He tucked the invitation back into the small envelope, laid it aside, then read the letter. After he finished, he walked to the front of the store and looked out at the empty street. An autumn wind was swirling dust through the deserted buildings. Nate stared at the bleak scene for a few moments, looking for former customers who would never come again. With a sigh, he lumbered back to the counter and took writing paper from beneath it, found pen and ink, then began to compose a response, speaking the words as he wrote slowly.

Dear Matt,

I know it ain't right to open other folk's mail but I took the liberty of doing it because Mr. and Mrs. Tom Patterson no longer live hereabouts and there was little chance that your letter would reach them. A circuit riding preacher married them a few weeks after you went home. Joe gave the bride away, I was Tom's best man, and the girls from the Gold Strike was there for Miss Betty.

Sorry to say they never finished fixing up the burned-down ranch, but decided to get a fresh start out in California, somewhere's that nobody would know about them. I know they'd be mighty pleased to hear about your coming wedding to your Miss Carpenter. I know they'd feel honored that you wanted them to come. I only wish I knew where to forward this invite, but I ain't yet heard where they've gone. Somewhere's near San Francisco where they was intending to buy a nice little place close to the big ocean.

I'm sure you'd be interested in some things that happened in the past two years. We heard that Dutch Snyder came to a bad end in another mining camp about three months after you left. He was hit in the head with a pick by a little miner he was beating on. The miners council decided it was self-defense and they let the fellow go.

To everyone's surprise, Joe Calvecci up and sold the Gold Strike one day when business was good and the town was booming. He, J. C., Wanda, Leann and Pauline all left town for parts

Jerry S. Drake

unknown. I guess he knew what he was doing because it wasn't but a few weeks later that the silver miners decided not to come to Gold Stream. The poor fellow that bought the Gold Strike closed down last month as have most of the other places of business. We still have a few folks trying to pan for gold around here, but most have moved on to other places like Nevada and California.

As for me, I'm still making something of a living taking care of people who've deciding that ranching will be the future here. There's talk of changing the town name when they get around to making this a real town. There's thinking of calling it Mountain View or Pleasant City or even name it after some dead president.

Whatever they decide, if the town don't blow away, I'm sure it will be nice and respectable with churches and schools and proper folk going to both. I'll kinda miss the good old days when it was sort of wild and lively.

I'd like to offer my congrats to you and your new bride. I hope your life together will be as happy as Tom and Miss Betty's. Just as soon as they send me their address . . .

Nate looked up at the sound of the door opening and saw a man and a woman with three small children entering the store.

"Can I help you?" he called.

The husky young man walked forward and spoke in a polite, resolute manner. "I wonder if I could get some information," he began, gesturing to his family. "I'm

Bob Wilson out of Tennessee. This is my wife, Nora, and my children." He paused. "We're fixing to settle in this area and we wondered if you might know of a parcel of land that might be for sale?"

Nate brightened and a smile came across his face. "That's welcome news, sir," he said cordially, nodding to the woman. "Mrs. Wilson, pleased to meet you and your young 'uns." He turned back to the young man. "I'm Nathan Wainscote. It's good that we might have some new folks coming into the territory." He paused, then continued, "I do know of a pretty place not far out of town. Already got a start on a house on the property. As a matter of fact, I've been asked by a friend to represent that property."

"It couldn't be too expensive," the young man said.

"No, no, not at all," Nate said soothingly. "I'm sure we could give you a good price on it." He came out from behind the counter, offering his huge hand.

The man smiled broadly and shook Nate's hand. "Sounds promising," he said. "What's life like around here?"

"Oh, it's nice and peaceful," Nate said. "Getting better all the time. You folks get settled in and I 'spect you've got kinfolk and friends back there in Tennessee who'd love to come out and make a good life for themselves."

"Might at that," the young man agreed. "Would it be much trouble if we could see that place?"

"No trouble at all," Nate replied. "Just give me a couple of minutes to finish up what I was doing."

The man nodded and escorted his family from the store to the wagon outside. Nate walked back to the counter, took up his pen again, dipped the nib in the inkwell and started writing.

> ... *I'll forward it to you. If you ever get to California, somewhere's south of San Francisco, I'm sure Tom and Betty would love to see you and your new missus. As for Gold Stream, by whatever name, I reckon somehow, someway, we'll still be here. If you happen to pass this way, I'd be happy to see you and the missus and talk about old times. Pleased to have been your friend,*
> *Nathan Wainscote*

Nate blotted the ink on the bottom of the page, folded the letter and stuffed it into an envelope. He copied the return address from Matt's letter onto the envelope, then laid it on the counter. "Send it on the next mail," he said to himself.

He turned away and started for the front door, whistling a tune he'd often heard played on the piano at the Gold Strike. He stepped outside, locked the door, and hauled his heavy bulk up onto the rear of the wagon to sit with the Wilson children, asking their names. Then, he turned to their parents and pointed the way west.